A RYAN CHRISTMAS

NEW YORK RUTHLESS SHORT STORIES

SADIE KINCAID

RED HOUSE PRESS

For my beautiful Fin, who is where this all began. You turned our worlds upside down and changed the course of my life forever. But I would give it all up for just one Christmas with you.

And, as always, for my readers.
Merry Christmas
Sadie xxx

NEW YORK RUTHLESS

This is a novella connected to the New York Ruthless series, set after the end of Ryan Renewed. It is a dark Mafia, reverse harem romance which deals with adult themes including scenes of an explicit sexual nature.

If you haven't read the series yet, you can find them on Amazon and Kindle Unlimited

Ryan Rule

Ryan Redemption

Ryan Retribution

Ryan Reign

Ryan Renewed

New York Ruthless short stories/ novellas can be found here

A Ryan Reckoning

A Ryan Rewind

A Ryan Halloween

CHAPTER
ONE
JESSIE

Five days to Christmas

My fingers are trembling as I press the button for the elevator of our penthouse apartment. If I just keep taking deep breaths, I'll be okay, right?

You can do this, Jessie. Just breathe. It's all gonna be fine.

"Where did you say you were headed, angel?" His deep voice carries across the hallway.

Shit!

I have four husbands, Shane, Conor, Liam and Mikey Ryan. Of all of them, he had to be the one to come out here and ask me that They're pretty much all possessive alpha-holes who like to be made aware of my every move. I also suspect they all know me better than I even know myself, but Conor – well he sees right through me, no matter what.

Taking a breath in and forcing a smile, I turn and face him. "I told you. I'm not leaving the building. I'm going to the basement. I'm going to be perfectly safe."

1

He narrows his dark brown eyes at me as he steps closer. "Yeah, I heard that part. But why?"

"I also told you all it was something I had to do. It's Christmas related," I remind him. "I'll be back up here in two hours."

My breath stutters in my throat as he reaches me. I turn my head, averting my eyes from his intense gaze, but he catches my jaw in his fingers, tilting my chin so there is no escaping him.

"Why are you trembling, angel?" he growls and the sound travels through my bones.

Damn! Now I feel sick too.

"I-I'm not," I stammer. *Idiot!*

His jaw ticks as he glares at me. He knows I'm hiding something from him. Even if I wasn't shaking like a leaf in the fall, he would know.

"What are you up to, Jessie?" his already deep voice drops an octave, making a shiver skitter along my spine.

I gasp in a breath and an unexpected tear pricks at my eyes. I so wanted to do this. It was supposed to be a surprise. I imagined their faces when I showed them and how brave they would say I was to finally overcome my phobia of needles.

"I was going to get a tattoo," I whisper.

His handsome features are pulled into a frown. Relaxing his grip on my jaw, he brushes a single tear from my cheek with the pad of his thumb. "A tattoo? In the basement?"

"Yeah," I sniff. "Gia is downstairs. Chester let her in for me."

"Gia?"

"Yeah." Chester is one of our security detail, and Gia Fenton is the woman who did most of Conor's and his brothers' tattoos. Her designs are stunning and she is a true artist. When I spoke to her about the idea I had, she came up with a beautiful, simple design that would take no more than ninety minutes to complete. I figured I could handle that, but my needle phobia has other ideas. "I don't think I can do it though. And it was going to be so good too."

I reach into the pocket of my sweater dress and pull out the sketch she made me. Handing it to Conor, I watch as he unfolds the small piece of paper. It's a simple rose, but the thorns are his and his brother's names. They wind around the flower, furling into each other until they reach the top where our children's names, Ella and Finn, are the petals.

"Fuck. It would look incredible on you," he whispers, looking between me and the paper in his hand.

"It'd beautiful, right?"

"But you hate needles?"

"I know. That's why it's just simple black ink. She said the coloring in takes longer. I thought I could..." a sob wells up in my throat.

He places a strong hand on the back of my neck — both calming and possessive. "You want to do this, angel?" he asks as he hands me back my sketch.

"Yeah."

"Then let's do it. I'll be with you every second, okay? I'll hold your hand, or whatever you need."

I rest my forehead on his chest and suck in a breath, letting his comforting scent wash over and through me. As though somehow I can take some of his strength and imbibe it into my bones.

"I would never let anyone hurt you," he says, running his hands over my arms before pressing a soft kiss on the top of my head.

I know that he speaks the truth. My fear of needles is rooted in the fact that I have been stuck with them, drugged and kidnapped more times than any one person should ever have to. I mean most people go through their entire lives without having that happen, right? Not me.

3

This must be hard for him too. It would be so much easier for him to tell me that I don't need to do this. He could go and pay Gia for her time and tell her that I've changed my mind. Then he and I could curl up on the sofa and watch a Christmas movie. That would be the easy option. Easier for both of us. His instinct is to protect me. But he knows that what I need is for him to push me to be better. Stronger. Faster. No longer afraid. It's why he and his younger brother almost kill me in the gym four times a week.

"You'll hold me the whole time?" I whisper.

"Anything you need, angel."

AFTER CONOR TOLD his brothers he'd be accompanying me to the basement for a couple of hours, we headed down to his office in the nightclub which makes up the lower floors of this building. Gia is already set up when we walk inside.

"Hey," she greets me, arching an eyebrow as she sees Conor walk into the room behind me. No doubt wondering why he's here when I made her promise that this would be our secret.

"I need him to hold my hand," I explain with a wince, feeling foolish that I'm being such a baby about a needle.

"I figured you might need some back up," she says with a chuckle. "You couldn't even watch Liam getting his last tattoo."

"I know." I place a hand over my mouth as the memory makes me want to hurl. He was in the chair for six hours and I had to leave after fifteen minutes.

"I'm proud of you, girl," she adds. "Getting a tattoo when you're terrified of needles is a big deal. You're a fucking warrior."

"Yeah, well I don't feel like one," I whisper as I eye her instruments.

A wave of nausea washes over me and I sway on my feet.

Conor's warm hands grip my waist and he moves his lips close to my ear. "You're okay. You got this."

"Uh-huh," I mumble, not as convinced as he is.

"Just sit yourself down here," Gia says, patting the seat of Conor's large office chair.

I look at the chair and then at her, and then her needles.

Fuck! I'm going to pass out.

Heat creeps over my skin and perspiration prickles over my brow. I stand rooted to the spot.

Gia looks past me at Conor. "How about I give Conor here a little ink to start with and you can watch exactly what happens this time. Okay?" she suggests.

"Yeah," I breathe out the word. Knowing exactly what to expect will calm my nerves — won't it?

"Where do you want it, big guy?" she says with a grin.

If I wasn't about to throw up into her lap, I might give her some sass for flirting with my husband. Gia flirts with every single person she meets — no matter their gender or sexuality.

Conor pulls his t-shirt off over his head and tosses it onto his desk before taking a seat on the chair. He taps his collarbone, right next to the tattoo of my name. "Right here. Give me a heart next to Jessie."

She grins at me as she picks up her artists needle. "You watching closely?"

I step closer to Conor and he reaches for my hand, lacing his fingers through mine. When Gia pierces his skin for the first time, I flinch but Conor doesn't even flicker. He winks at me as he squeezes my hand in his.

"Just a scratch. It doesn't go all that deep, see?" he nods toward Gia's hand as she draws over and over the tiny heart.

"Yeah," I whisper.

He knows I'm not afraid of pain. It is the act of the needle piercing my skin that terrifies me.

I force myself to watch as Gia drags the needle repeatedly over Conor's skin to create a small heart the size of a pea. A few minutes later, she sits back with a proud smile on her face. "Not bad for freehand, right?"

Conor looks down at his tiny new ink. "Hmm," he nods his agreement before he looks back at me. "You ready, angel?"

"Uh-huh," I murmur but I stand rooted to the spot.

"Where are you having your tattoo?" he asks.

"On m-my shoulder."

He tugs my hand, still clasped in his. "Come here." His words are soft but his tone is commanding and my body obeys him even though my brain is telling me to run from the room and far away from the small pointy instruments of torture.

I edge closer until my thighs are touching his.

"Here!" he looks down at his lap.

With shaky legs, I straddle him on the chair, placing my hands on his solid chest and feeling how he grounds me. My fingertips flex over the tattoos on his chest. The myriad of dark colors swirling and coiling into beautiful patterns on his skin.

Grabbing hold of my waist, he shifts his position slightly. "You okay there?" he asks.

I swallow hard. My groin is directly over his cock and the memories of the many times I have sat with him like this on this chair makes wet heat pool in my core.

"Yes," I whisper as I stare into his eyes.

He sees it too, as though he's watching the thoughts in my head like a movie. His eyes darken as a low growl rumbles through his chest.

"You wanna take your dress off or just pop your arm out, Jessie?" Gia asks as she readies her equipment for her next victim — me.

"Arm out," Conor growls, glaring at me in warning. "I'm barely gonna get through this with you fully clothed."

Despite my nerves, that makes me giggle. I pull my arm through my sweater dress and pull down my bra strap, exposing my right shoulder to be Gia's canvas.

When she wipes my skin with alcohol a few seconds later, the unexpected touch of her fingers on me makes me instinctively edge forward, causing me to rub my pussy over Conor's cock.

"Fuck!" he hisses.

"Sorry. Should have warned you," Gia laughs softly.

"That's okay," I reply, my eyes locked on Conor's.

His length hardens against me until it's nudging at my folds through my panties. Under almost any other circumstances that would be enough to distract me from anything. And I want to focus only on the feel of his body against mine, but the familiar feelings of pleasure, comfort and warmth that he usually evokes remain frustratingly close, yet too far to reach.

I FLINCH every single time Gia touches my skin and the longer she works, the more my entire body starts to tremble with fear.

"You're gonna have to do something to calm your girl, down, Conor," she says with a sigh. "She's shaking like a goddam jell-o shot in a virgin's belly button here."

I understand what she's saying but I can't stop my body from quivering. I need something to focus on. Something to distract me. Something all consuming.

"What do you suggest, Gia?" he says as his fingertips dig into the soft flesh of my hips.

"Whatever she needs, right?" she purrs while I stare into Conor's eyes, hoping he's willing to go that far.

His cock twitches against me and I roll my hips just the tiniest amount but it's enough to make me whimper with need.

Gia puts her instruments down on the metal tray with a

clatter. "I tell you what's gonna happen. I'm gonna go use the ladies room. And when I come back you two can be in whatever *situation* you need to be in to make this happen. Okay."

"Situation?" Conor snaps at her. "Are you-?"

"I don't care what you do, man. Pretty sure I have already seen and done everything that you are worrying about right now. Just get your girl to relax so we can get this done, because right now she has half a tattoo and we've been at this for almost an hour. Okay?"

Then without another word, she walks out of the office to find the ladies room, leaving Conor and me alone.

"Tell me what you need, angel," he breathes.

I bear down on him, pressing my aching pussy against his cock and making heat sear between my thighs. "This, Conor," I whimper. "I need to get out of my head."

"Fuck!" he mutters. "You know if Shane were here with you now, he'd already be inside you?"

"I know," I say with a smile. His older brother would love to fuck me with an audience, but Conor has always been so against it that Shane has held off from doing it so far. "But I'm still glad it's you here with me."

"Fuck! You know I'll always give you what you need," he grinds out the words as though they pain him to say.

"I know that."

He pinches the bridge of his nose. "So take off the damn panties," he says with a deep sigh that rolls through his entire body.

"Are you sure?"

"I don't think this tattoo is gonna get finished otherwise, is it?"

"Probably not," I admit.

"So do as you're told and take off your panties," he growls as his hard cock twitches against me.

I climb off him and reach beneath my sweater dress. Hooking my fingers into my panties, I peel them off over my legs.

"Give them to me," Conor orders and I place them in his outstretched palm.

He wads them into a ball and stuffs them into the pocket of his sweatpants. Reaching for my hand again, he pulls me back onto his lap. "Take what you need, angel," he growls.

Reaching between us, I tug his sweatpants down and release his huge cock. The crown glistens with precum and I bite back a smile but he sees it anyway.

"You seriously think having you sitting on my lap, grinding yourself on my cock would have me any other way, Jessie?" he groans. "Now slide your hot pussy onto me before Gia comes back in here."

I wrap my hand around his thick shaft, causing a deep groan to rumble through his chest, before sinking onto him. He slides easily into my wet heat and I sink all the way down until our bodies are flush together. The sensation of being so full of him makes warmth and relief curl around my spine and flutter through my body.

"You feel so good," I hiss as I roll my hips over him.

"Fuck!" he mutters, his teeth catching on his bottom lip as he grabs my waist and holds me still. "You can't ride me while you're getting a tattoo, Jessie, you're gonna have to stay still."

"I know," I whimper as a rush of wet heat slicks us both. "But I'm not getting a tattoo right this second."

The sound of the door opening makes Conor's grip on me tighten and I close my eyes and still my hips. Despite how much I want to grind on him right now, I know that he's right and I need to remain as still as possible while Gia has the instrument of torture pressed against my back. And having him inside me is calming enough for now.

"We ready to proceed?" Gia asks with a knowing smile. She can't see thanks to my dress — but, oh she knows - if only by the pained expression on Conor's face.

"Yep," I say.

"Uh-huh," Conor grunts, narrowing his eyes at me in warning.

I bite my lip to stop myself from laughing at the look on his face but at least it distracts me from Gia's needles and I barely even notice when she starts tattooing me again.

I concentrate on Conor's fingers digging into my hips. His huge cock throbbing inside my pussy as I force myself to keep still. But then as Gia switches from the quiet pen back to her gun, the sound of the tiny motor makes me flinch.

"It's okay, angel," Conor says softly, his deep voice rolling through my core.

But my body starts to tremble slightly.

"Keep her still," Gia warns.

His gaze holds mine as he slides his hand beneath my dress and starts to rub the pad of his thumb softly over my clit, making endorphins flood my body.

I hiss out a breath but it stops the trembling as I focus on his expert fingers soothing me. He doesn't apply enough pressure to get me off yet, just enough to make the pleasure coil up my spine and into every nerve ending in my body.

My walls squeeze around him and a growl rumbles through his chest. "Don't," he warns me.

I stare at him, my eyelids fluttering as he goes on gently rubbing my clit.

"Hold it, Jessie," he grinds out the words.

I smile at him. He thinks I'm the only one about to come. That is so sweet.

I squeeze my walls around him again and again. Squeezing

and releasing. Over and over. I see his eyes rolling in his head as he fights to maintain control.

"Jessie!" he hisses, but it's too late. My walls ripple around him as I bring us both to the edge.

His eyes press tightly closed and his jaw sets in a grimace, his fingers digging deeper into the soft flesh of my hips as he comes inside me with a deep, but almost silent grunt. And the sight of my usually cool, calm husband losing control tips me over the edge too. With his strong hands holding me, I manage to stay completely still while my orgasm rolls through my body in a long, intense wave. I clamp my lips together to stop myself from moaning loudly and the effort of staying still and quiet makes the climax even more intense. It implodes inside me, sending aftershocks of pleasure skittering through all of my nerve endings.

A tiny whimper escapes and I hold my breath, wondering if Gia is going to laugh or give any indication that she knows what just happened, but she goes on working diligently on my tattoo — seemingly lost in her art and being a complete professional.

CHAPTER

TWO

CONOR

S taring up at my deviant wife, I watch the relief wash over her beautiful face as Gia finally says those words she's been waiting for.

"All done."

"Really?" Jessie breathes.

"Yup." Gia holds up a small mirror and Jessie cranes her neck so she can see the work of art that's just been permanently tattooed onto her shoulder. I look too. It's fucking perfect, just like her.

"Oh," Jessie gasps. "I love it, Gia. It's beautiful."

"It looks hot," Gia says with a proud grin. "Just let me cover it."

Gia cleans Jessie up and takes a clear plastic wrap that's also used for burns from the table beside her and places it on Jessie's shoulder. She always covers her tattoos with them and they work way more effectively than anything else I've seen. You just leave it on for a few days and then peel it off, leaving a perfect tattoo with no scabbing.

The smile on Jessie's face makes my cock throb inside her. I'm so fucking proud of her. I'm also pissed that she made us both come in front of Gia. I mean what the fuck was that thing she did with the squeezing? I had no fucking control at all. She took it all.

She played me.

She looks down at me, her face flushed pink and her eyes shining with happiness. My cock is still inside her and I'm still hard as fuck.

"Gia, I'm gonna need you to go," I grunt.

"Okay," she says as she starts collecting her stuff. "So, Jessie, you're gonna need to-"

"Now, Gia!"

She turns and blinks at me. "I need to go through the aftercare."

"Pretty sure I know how to take care of a tattoo," I breathe out the words as my fingers dig into Jessie's hips. Half my body is covered in ink.

"Fine," she says with a sigh and roll of her eyes. "Just let me get my stuff."

"I'll have someone bring it to your studio," I hiss, making Jessie giggle softly.

"Whatever," she says with a shrug. "This was my last job before the holidays anyway. Have someone deliver it after ten tonight, yeah?"

"Will do," I say, staring into Jessie's bright blue eyes. She licks her lip and my balls twitch.

"Okay, well, Happy holidays, I guess," Gia says with a soft laugh.

"Bye, Gia. Happy holidays and thanks again," Jessie says sweetly, as though she's not currently gripping my cock in her pussy.

"You're welcome, girl."

"Go!" I bark.

"I'm going," Gia sighs and then makes her way out of my office. She turns and winks at Jessie before she leaves.

As soon as the door is closed I sigh with relief. "You are so gonna pay for that," I say, grabbing the edge of Jessie's dress and pulling it off over her head.

"Pay for what?" she purrs, fluttering her eyelashes at me.

God, I fucking love her. "For making me come in front of Gia."

She doesn't deny it. Instead she bites on her bottom lip and I can't take another damn second of her teasing. Grabbing onto her hips, I push myself up out of the chair, my cock still inside her as I walk her to my desk.

She wraps her legs around my waist and I narrow my eyes at her, brushing a loose wave of her hair behind her ear. "Did you just fuck me?"

She raises her eyebrows in amusement. "Kinda."

"You know that is not how this works, right? I fuck you, angel."

"Yeah?" she stares into my eyes, challenging me. The fear that she felt just two hours ago completely dissipated now. And I can't even describe how much I love that I can do that for her.

"Yeah," I growl as I pull her off my cock and spin her around, bending her over my desk.

I push her thighs apart with my knee and take a second to stare at her almost naked body. She's only wearing knee high boots and a bra. Her sweet pussy is dripping with our cum. Wet, warm and pink, and begging to be filled. Then there's her ass. Her perfect peach of an ass. I swear half the time I don't know whether to eat it or worship it.

I rub my hand over it and she shivers. "You need me to remind you who is in control here, angel?"

It's her. It's always fucking her. One word and I would be on my knees at her feet and she knows it. But that she allows me the illusion that it's me is one of the many, many reasons I adore her.

"You are," she whimpers. "I'm sorry."

"It's a bit late for sorry now, Jessie," I growl as I open my desk drawer and pull out my belt. I keep it in here as a spare — for occasions like this when I'm not wearing one and I want to spank her beautiful ass.

"Conor," she moans softly as she hears the familiar jingle of the belt buckle.

I spank her with my hand first, leaving a satisfying red hand print on her skin as she hisses out a breath.

"Why did you make me come even when I warned you not to?" I ask as I bring my hand down again.

"I couldn't help it," she giggles, making me spank her harder.

"And now you're lying to me?"

"I-I," she stammers. "I really couldn't stop."

"You could, you just didn't want to." Palming the buckle, I wrap the leather around my fist. "Isn't that right?" The belt slices through the air as I bring it down over her ass cheeks with a satisfying crack.

"Ah," she cries, wriggling her ass until I spank her again.

"Answer the question, Jessie."

"Yes," she moans. "I didn't want to stop."

Crack!

"So why did you disobey me, angel?"

Crack!

"Because I wanted to see you lose control," she whispers, half giggling despite the fact she has pink and white stripes all over her backside.

"And how has that worked out for you?"

Crack!

"Pretty damn perfect if I'm honest," she breathes as she closes her eyes and presses her face against the desk.

I can't help but smile at her. My horny little angel.

I drop my belt to the floor, desperate now to fuck her. Pressing my hands on the tops of her thighs and her ass cheeks, I spread her wide open for me and she shivers at my touch.

"You're so fucking beautiful," I whisper as I push two fingers inside her.

"Please, Conor," she whimpers as I finger fuck her slowly, readying her for the absolute pounding I'm about to give her.

Only when her thighs are trembling and she's whimpering with need do I pull my fingers out and drive my cock into her instead. She cries out my name and it makes my balls tighten.

I bury myself in her. Over and over again. Driving further and harder inside her.

Bending her over always allows for hitting that sweet spot deep in her pussy that makes her come real hard. I fuck her until our bodies are slick with perspiration and our thighs are wet with her juices. I've made her come already but she's teetering on the edge again. She squeezes me tight, wanting to take me with her.

"Conor," she breathes out my name as another orgasm rolls through her body, softer this time. Her eyes roll in her head as she rides the waves and I thrust deeper as my own climax tears through me, searing heat in my balls and my spine.

I lean over her, careful to avoid the hot, tender skin where she just got her first tattoo and press my lips against her ear. "I'm so fucking proud of you, angel."

"Thank you for making me strong enough to go through with it," she whispers.

"You were already strong enough. You just needed a little reminder, is all."

. . .

CHAPTER TWO

When we walk back into the apartment, we head for the kitchen where my brothers are gathered with our babies. Ella is crawling around the floor with Liam while Finn sits quietly on Shane's lap playing with a toy cell phone.

"Where have you two been for so long?" Mikey asks with a frown.

He's making dinner and wearing his Kiss the Chef apron.

"I got a surprise," Jessie says excitedly.

"What?" my three brothers say in unison.

She walks over to Shane who is closest and pulls down the sleeve of her sweater dress to reveal her brand new tattoo.

"You got a tattoo?" Liam asks, scooping Ella up before he walks over to her. He traces his fingertips lightly over the plastic wrap.

"Is that all of our names?" Mikey asks as he comes closer and peers at her shoulder with a huge goofy smile on his face.

"Yes." She smiles back at him.

"It's beautiful, baby," Liam says, kissing her shoulder softly.

She looks at Shane, waiting for his reaction. "You got a tattoo?" he eventually asks.

"Yep." She blinks at him, desperate for his approval too.

His brow furrows in confusion and then he looks at me. "You fucked her while she was getting a tattoo."

I swallow while Jessie's mouth hangs open in shock. "How do you even know that?" she says. "Did you watch on the security camera?"

"No," he shakes his head and laughs. "But you are terrified of needles, sweetheart, and that is the quickest and surest way I know to calm you down."

"True," Mikey adds with a nod.

Shane is staring at me again, a wicked glint in his eyes. I groan inwardly because I know what he's thinking.

"So you did fuck her?" he asks.

17

"Yeah," I sigh. Closing my eyes to avoid the smug look on his face.

"You fucked our wife and made her come in front of another person?"

"It was Gia," Jessie adds, as though that somehow makes this better.

"Interesting," he says with a nod as he slips an arm around her waist. "Your tattoo is beautiful by the way, sweetheart. I love it." He kisses her shoulder softly and she beams with pride.

"This doesn't mean it's open season for you two to go nailing our wife in public," I say to Shane and Mikey who are exchanging glances that let me know that is exactly what they are thinking about.

"You started it, bro. You fucked Jessie in front of Gia," Mikey replies, his arms crossed over his chest.

"Can we all stop saying the word 'fuck' in front of our children?" I suggest as Finn and Ella stare up at us.

"Yes," Jessie agrees.

"So what do we say?" Liam asks with a frown.

I look around the kitchen and suggest the first object that grabs my attention. "Balloon?"

"So you ballooned Jessie in front of Gia then?" Mikey says with a grin, making Jessie and Liam snigger.

"Actually, it was more like Jessie ballooned me," I reply.

"How is that?" Shane asks.

Liam raises his eyebrows. "Oh, she do that squeezing thing?"

"You know about that?" I ask him.

"Course," he says with a shrug.

"What squeezing thing?" Shane demands as he looks between me and her.

"Ah, the squeezing," Mikey says with a contented sigh.

"What is this fu-" Shane starts to say before he remembers

the 'no fuck' rule we just made, "ballooning squeezing are you talking about?" His scowl deepens.

Jessie laughs harder, placing her hand on his face. "You wouldn't know about this because you never, ever, give up enough control to let me do it to you," she says with a shrug. "Neither does Conor usually."

I nod my agreement. I have never been so still inside her that she's been able to do that to me before. Unless she's sucking my cock, I'm all about making her come, not the other way around.

"So, what is it?" Shane snaps.

"So, basically while you're... ballooning," I laugh now. I couldn't have chosen a better word? "You stay completely still and Jessie just squeezes and releases until..."

"Until..." Mikey mimes an explosion.

"Like the fourth of July," Liam adds.

"It was pretty intense," I agree.

Shane narrows his eyes at her. "I need to try this, sweetheart."

"I doubt you could handle it," she whispers in his ear and the vein in his neck starts to bulge. I swear if he wasn't holding our son he would bend her over the breakfast island, spank her and then fuck her.

A timer goes off behind us. "Dinner is ready," Mikey declares. "Sit your asses down and let's eat."

"Saved by the bell, Jessie," Shane says, scowling at her.

She takes his face in her hands and kisses him softly. "I can show you later if you like though."

"I have to work after dinner."

"Perfect. I'll help you. And then..."

"Fourth of July," he finishes for her, smacking her on the ass before he walks to the dinner table.

THREE
JESSIE

4 days to Christmas

Conor frowns as he listens to whoever is talking on the other end of his cell phone.

"You've tried everyone?" he asks with a sigh. "For fuck's sake, isn't this why I pay you, Bianca? To manage?"

A few seconds later, he says. "Leave it with me," before ending the call.

"Problem?" Shane asks.

"Apparently half of the bar staff have some kind of stomach bug meaning we are seriously short staffed. It's Christmas week and the place is going to be busting at the seams with no fucker to serve them."

"I could work the bar," I suggest.

"No," Conor snaps.

"What?" I ask with a frown. "I've worked in bars for years. I know what I'm doing. At least it's one more body down there."

"Maybe I don't want your body down there," Conor says making Shane chuckle.

"Oh, don't be ridiculous. I'll be perfectly safe. It's your club. One of you can even come be my bodyguard for the night."

"I'll watch her," Shane offers.

"If she's going to work in our club, don't you think I should watch her?"

"No, because you will snarl at every guy she serves and end up throat punching half of them," Shane replies.

"True," I say with a smile.

"And you won't?" Conor challenges him.

"Anyone makes a pass at her and they'll get a punch in the mouth, but asking her for a drink I can handle."

"So, it's settled then. Tell Bianca I'll help out. I'll start at ten and stay until they need me."

Conor frowns as he considers my request.

"All hell will break loose down there if people can't get their beer," Shane says. "I'll take care of her."

"Fine," Conor grunts as he calls the manager of our night-club back.

"Thank you," I whisper to Shane who winks at me.

I'm actually looking forward to a night behind the bar. I always loved working in them when I was younger. I love drunk people. I love the club. I love Christmas. What could possibly go wrong?

CLOSING THE CASH REGISTER, I turn back to the sea of faces waiting to be served at the bar. I've been down here for three hours now and the club just keeps getting busier and busier. I, along with the other bar staff, have been working flat out to keep up with the rush.

I love it though. The music. The buzz of it all.

"Jessie? Jessie Heaton is that you?" A voice that sounds vaguely familiar shouts loudly. Turning to face the direction of the noise, I see a guy with a dark goatee wearing a Santa hat.

"It's me, Jason," he says with a big grin, launching himself across the bar with his arms wide open as though he's about to drag me in for a hug.

He is stopped by a large hand grabbing the scruff of his neck, pulling him sharply backward and making him yelp in surprise. That's when I realize who I'm looking at. Jason Donegan. I haven't seen him in ten years. A ghost of Christmas past if ever there was one.

"What the hell, man?" he snaps at Shane who glares at him, practically foaming at the mouth.

"You do not fucking touch her," he snarls. "Never fucking touch her."

Jason shrugs himself free from Shane's grip. "Who are you? Her bodyguard?"

Oh, crap!

Shane's jaw is clenched tightly shut and I see the telltale drawing back of his shoulders. Jason is about to get a punch in the mouth — or much worse. But the club is packed. It's almost Christmas. Everyone is drunk and happy — the last thing we need is my possessive husband tearing off someone's head at the bar.

"Jason, this is my husband, Shane," I shout, wishing I could get out there and stand between the two of them and diffuse some of the anger that is radiating from Shane in waves. But two feet of mahogany and ebony is in my way. I reach out instead, placing my hand on Shane's arm.

Jason holds his hands up in surrender. "I just wanted to say hello. I knew Jessie way back, is all," he says.

"I don't give a fuck when you knew her, or how, you do not

touch what belongs to me," Shane snarls. "Touch her and I will break your hand. Do you fucking understand me?"

"She's not your property, man," Jason scowls at him.

"Shane?" I plead. "He's just an old..." I stumble over the word. Fuck, what is he? "Friend," I finally say. Deciding that is the best description I can offer right now.

Shane grabs him by his collar. "She *is* my property, asshole. Every single inch of her. So stay the fuck away." He pushes Jason backward and a few seconds later he's swallowed by the huge crowd.

I roll my eyes, watching the Santa hat bobbing away through the throngs of people. When I look back at Shane, he is glaring at me, his eyes narrowed. "Who was that asshole?"

"Just some guy I knew a long time ago," I say with a shrug before I look at the woman dressed as a sexy Mrs. Claus who has just sidled up next to up him, and is waiting to be served.

"Knew him how?" Shane asks, speaking loudly enough that I can hear him in the club, but somehow keeping that low, menacing tone that turns my insides to warm butter, and also lets me know that this conversation isn't over.

I glance back at him, unable to stop my eyebrows from pulling my face into a frown even though I don't want to start anything with him right now. But I don't know what to say. I can't lie to him, but if I tell him the truth he might just run after Jason, pull off his arms and beat him to death right on the middle of the dance floor.

I falter for way too long before I reply. "I stayed with him for a few weeks one Christmas, that's all. There's nothing else to know."

Then I turn back to sexy Mrs. Claus. "What can I get you?"

Clearly that is not an acceptable answer to my husband's question and the next thing I know, he is vaulting the bar like a goddamn Olympic gymnast. Mrs. Claus stares at him open mouthed — a mixture of surprise, awe and desire on her face. I mean he is a pretty fine ass man and he just cleared a bar in one jump to get to me.

"Sha-" I don't even get his full name out of my mouth before he is on me. One hand gripping my waist and one in my hair as he crashes his lips over mine, making my legs tremble. His kiss is brief but full of fire and when he pulls back I'm left gasping. The fact that he only did it to mark his territory, showing everyone in this club who I belong to, doesn't make it any less hot.

He takes my hand and pulls me to the room behind the bar where the glasses are washed. He leads me to the back toward the storeroom, ignoring the looks of surprise on the two young glass collector's faces as they pass us with full trays. Once we're inside the small room, he closes the door.

I take a step back, pressing myself flat against the wall and trying to create a little space between us in this tiny room, because he looks a little pissed right now.

"Who is he?" he demands.

I fight every instinct in my body, willing my eyes not to roll — but they do anyway. Damn!

"Did you just...?" he snarls, advancing on me until he has me pinned against the wall. Placing one of his huge hands on the back of my neck, he runs the pad of his thumb along the curve of my jaw, causing goosebumps to break out all over my body.

He sucks in a breath and licks his lip, trying to control his temper. Meanwhile I'm trying to control the urge to push his buttons even more and make him fuck me over a stack of beer. It would be exactly what we both need right now, but I have to get back out to the bar before the crowd become a baying mob. There's nothing as demanding as a bunch of drunk people at Christmas, who are intent on getting even more drunk.

"Do not make me ask again," he says quietly, but there is no mistaking the threat implicit in his tone.

"His name is Jason. I met him in Virginia and I stayed with him for a few weeks when I needed a place to crash."

"How many weeks?"

"Six."

"Did you fuck him?"

"Yes," I whisper, trying to avoid his intense gaze but being unable to.

He narrows his eyes at me. "Okay. But I know you fucked other people before I met you, Jessie. Why are you being so vague about this guy? Did you love him?"

"God, no!" I wrinkle my face in disgust.

"So? Why so sketchy about him?" He pushes his body against mine, making warmth pool in my center and coil around my spine. He presses his thumb on my jawbone, tilting my chin slightly so he can stare directly into my eyes.

"I'm not being sketchy. I just don't want you to go all Shane on him, is all."

He frowns at my use of his name as an adjective. "I swear to God, if you don't tell me what the fuck happened between you two right now I will drag him in here and ask him myself. And you know I'm not gonna go about that politely."

"Promise you won't kill him?"

"Depends what he did."

I arch an eyebrow at him. "Nothing worth killing him for."

"I'll be the judge of that. Now talk."

"I was eighteen. It was a few weeks before Christmas. I needed a place to crash. I met him in a bar where I was working..."

Shane narrows his eyes in confusion.

"I pretended to be twenty-one. I had a fake ID, but the owners weren't the kind to check anyway — you know what I mean? As long as I was a hit with the customers and I didn't give them any trouble, they were happy to have me," I'm babbling now.

"You're stalling, sweetheart."

"I'm telling you how I met him," I say with a sigh and I don't miss the annoyance that flashes over his face. "So, I told Jason I needed a place to stay for the holidays and he offered me one. He seemed like a nice guy so I took it."

"And?"

I close my eyes and take a breath. This is the part he won't like. "After a day or two, it became clear that staying there came with some..." I struggle to find the right word for a few seconds, "expectations."

His frown deepens into a scowl. "He forced you to have sex with him?"

"I wouldn't say forced," I scrunch up my eyes. I am not handling this well at all. Jason is going to have his head on a spike if I don't stop making him sound like a rapist. "He just made some suggestions about what I could do to repay him for his kindness, and because I was trying to lie low, I went along with them. But I was a willing, if not enthusiastic, participant."

"He made you have sex so you could keep a roof over your head? That is not willing, Jessie," he snarls.

I cup his face in my hands. "No. He never threatened to throw me out. He just suggested that I could sleep in his bed and stuff..."

"Stuff?"

"You know what I mean, Shane. Besides, he didn't know I was on the run from the Wolf and how desperate I was for somewhere to stay. I genuinely think he thought he was helping me out and that I was into him. I mean, he was a nice looking guy with a nice place and a hot car. He was rich — or his parents were. I'm pretty sure he got laid whenever he wanted."

"Yet he still pressured young women into sex?"

"He's an asshole. He was then and no doubt he is now. Can we forget about him? Please?" I whisper, standing on my tiptoes to pepper soft kisses over his face.

He grunts his response, the hand on my neck now fisting in my hair while his free hand slides to my ass. He squeezes hard, making me moan, my lips twitching against his jaw. When he dips his head low and runs his nose over the soft skin of my throat, I whimper with need, rocking my hips and rubbing myself over his hardening cock.

"You belong to me, Jessie. Every fucking inch of you is mine."

"I know, Shane."

"How much longer do you need to work in this damn bar before I can take you to bed and fuck your brains out?"

Oh my God! "Until three, maybe? It should quiet down a little after that."

"Fuck. That's two more hours."

"I know." I grab hold of the lapels of his jacket, pulling him closer to me.

He growls in my ear, dragging my body over his thick cock as it bulges in his suit pants. "You make me feel like a goddamn animal."

"You are an animal," I whisper, dusting my lips over his. "And I can't wait for you to mount me later."

"Fuck, Jessie! You're not helping here," he groans loudly, making me giggle.

"Sorry. It's not exactly easy resisting you when you have me pinned against a wall with your huge cock. Not to mention having to watch women drool all over you while you sit at that bar."

He drags his teeth over the shell of my ear. "Sitting at that bar watching you," he whispers, making me shiver. "Besides, you think I like watching guys looking at your ass every single time you turn around? You wonder why all the guys ask for the Bud Light, sweetheart? It's because it's on the bottom shelf of the refrigerator and you have to bend to get it."

"Bud Light is just a very popular drink," I whisper, wrapping my arms around his neck.

"Really? If we don't get out of this room in the next five seconds, I'm gonna have to bend you over that stack of it, and you won't be going anywhere but bed because you won't be able to walk after. *One.*"

"That sounds kinda hot."

"*Two.*"

"How quick can you be, because I gotta get back to work?"

"*Three.*"

"You know that door has no lock, right?"

"*Four,*" he growls, his grip on me tightening.

I grab hold of his hand and pull him toward the door before he can get to five, opening it wide before he has a chance to pull me back inside and make good on his promise.

It's just before 3am. The club has quieted down a little and I figure the bar staff can manage without me for the next three hours.

Shane is deep in conversation with one of the club bouncers and I need to pee. I start to head in the direction of the ladies room.

"Where are you going?" he shouts after me.

I walk back to him because I don't want to announce to the

entire club where I'm headed. "I'm just going to the ladies room. Then I'll cash up my register and we can go home?"

"Give me two minutes and I'll come with you."

I cross my arms over my chest. "I need to pee. I can go to the bathroom on my own."

He looks to another bouncer who is standing nearby. "Watch her," he barks.

"I'll use the bathroom in Conor's office. It's like thirty feet away. I'll be fine," I say with a roll of my eyes.

He simply scowls at me in response as his employee talks in his ear about something which appears important. So I leave him to it and head off to the office with the other bouncer's eyes burning a hole into my skin.

I'm through the door when I feel someone behind me. A hand between my shoulder blades gently guiding me into the room.

"I can't believe you couldn't even let me go to the bathroom alone," I say with a chuckle as the door closes behind us. But when I turn around, it's not Shane who just shoved me into this room. "J-Jason," I stammer. "What the hell?"

He grabs my wrist, his fingers pressing into the soft skin of my forearm as he holds me a little too tight. His eyes are glassy but they are fixed on my face.

"Jessie," he says and there is something in his tone that I can't work out. "Are you okay?"

"Well, not right now, I'm not," I snap. "Get your damn hands off me."

He releases his grip at the same time as the pounding starts on the door behind him. Startled by the noise, Jason stumbles forward and onto me. He smells of alcohol and cigars and I wrinkle my nose at the offensive stench.

"Jessie! Open this fucking door!" Shane shouts while the banging continues.

I look behind Jason. "You need to open that door, right now," I say, aware of the tremor in my voice.

"Jessie. You're shaking," he reaches for me, brushing his fingertips over my cheek and making me flinch.

"Open this fucking door or I will tear your fucking head off!" Shane yells behind him.

Jason glances back quickly. "I can help you get away from him, Jessie. I know people."

I blink at him. "I don't want to get away from him. It's not my head he's about to tear off. What the hell are you talking about?"

The banging grows louder and the door rattles as though is about to come off its hinges.

"The way he talked about you," he says with a sneer. "You *belong* to him?"

"Jason. Listen to me. If you do not open that door right now and he has to break it down, he is going to kill you."

"I can protect us, baby," he whispers as he reaches for me again.

I dodge past him, elbowing him in the stomach as I run for the door and wrench it open, coming face to face with the wall of rage that is an incredibly pissed off Shane Ryan.

He pulls me straight into his arms, wrapping them tight around me and kissing my head. He walks into the room, kicking the door closed behind him and only then does he release me from his embrace. "Are you okay, sweetheart?"

"Yes, I'm fine," I say with a nod.

His eyes burn with anger again as he looks past me and at Jason. "What the fuck?" he snarls, his teeth bared.

"I-I," Jason stammers.

Meanwhile Shane's eyes drift back to me and his gaze lingers on the red fingerprints on my arm. "Did he fucking touch you?" he rages.

"He just grabbed me. I'm fine," I say, subconsciously rubbing at the skin.

"I was protecting her. She's fucking scared of you."

Jason may have well just poured gasoline over an open flame as Shane's anger rips through him like an inferno. In one swift move, he has Jason by the throat. Spinning him around, he presses him against the door.

"What did you just fucking say to me?"

"She's fucking scared of you," Jason snarls. "She was shaking when I came in here."

I close my eyes and pray for Jason to pass out or something because I cannot believe how one person can be so utterly stupid.

"Because you just locked her in a fucking room, you stupid cunt!" Shane squeezes Jason's throat tighter, making his face turn purple.

"She's not your property, man," Jason croaks. "You don't get to treat her like that."

Instead of tearing his throat out like I expected, Shane lets him go. And then he starts to laugh, and I can't imagine any scenario where this is a good thing.

"Come here, sweetheart," Shane says to me as Jason rubs at the raw skin on his throat.

Obediently, I take a few steps until I'm standing by his side.

"Tell this fuckwit who you belong to."

I look Jason in the eyes as I take hold of Shane's hand. "I belong to him and I like it that way. You're not rescuing me from him, asshole."

Jason blinks, looking between me and Shane.

"You think she's fucking scared of me?" Shane laughs again.

"She can say what she likes now, but she was trembling when she heard you coming through that door."

Shane grabs his throat again. "Yeah? That's because my girl

is a nice person and she doesn't want me to rip your fucking heart out and feed it to you while it's still beating," he snarls before pushing Jason onto a chair nearby.

Picking up some of the Christmas lights we had left over from decorating the club from the floor, Shane starts to wind the length around Jason's chest, tying him to the chair. He struggles and curses but he's no match for a determined Ryan brother and a moment later, Jason's arms are pinned to his sides and he's bound tightly.

He struggles for a few moments longer, panting for breath as he tries to work himself free. But Shane can tie a knot better than anyone else I know. I have had plenty of first hand experience of his binding skills and there is no way Jason is getting out of those Christmas lights unless Shane wants him to.

Finally, accepting defeat, he mutters under his breath and stops wriggling, glaring at the two of us instead.

"Shall I show you how scared my girl is of me, Jason?" Shane snarls, taking my hand and leading me over to the desk.

I swallow hard as his fingers grip mine, wondering what the hell is going through his devious mind.

He taps the edge of Conor's huge desk. "Sit here, sweetheart."

I look into his eyes, trying to read his mind, but I do as he tells me because I trust him completely. When I'm perched on the edge of the desk with my back to Jason, Shane presses his lips against my ear. "I won't let him see anything."

"Okay," I whisper.

He nudges my thighs apart with his knee until he's standing between them. Sliding one hand beneath my skirt and up my inner thigh, he keeps his eyes on Jason. Then he brushes his free hand up my arm and over the curve of my breast, pushing me slightly. "Lean back for me."

I plant my palms on the desk and lean back a little as his

hand between my thighs glides higher. When his fingertips brush my panties, my breath hitches in my throat. He tugs the fabric aside, sliding a finger through my slickness.

"So fucking wet," he hisses as he pushes one finger inside me.

"Shane," I moan softy as my walls ripple and squeeze around him.

"Fucking terrified of me, aren't you, sweetheart?" he chuckles darkly as he starts to lazily finger fuck me.

I tip my head back as the waves of pleasure start rolling through my core.

"You hear that, Jason?" Shane asks as adds another finger and the sound of my arousal fills the small room. "You hear how wet my girl is?" he growls as he drives deeper.

"Shane," I whimper, holding onto his forearm as he drives deeper, pressing against my walls and sending deep, throbbing pulses of ecstasy through me.

"Come here," he growls, wrapping an arm around my waist and pulling me close to him. He presses his lips against my ear. "You feel so fucking good squeezing my fingers, Jessie," he whispers as he pulls them out of me.

He keeps my body pressed tight against his but he is glaring at Jason. "You got a hard on for my girl, asshole?"

"Fuck you!" Jason spits.

Shane puts the fingers he just had inside me into his mouth and sucks them clean. "Fuck, you taste so good," he looks at me again for a second before training his glare back on the other side of the room. "You remember how sweet she tastes?"

My cheeks flame with heat and I scrunch my eyes closed because I can't believe we're about to have this conversation right now. "He never..." I whisper.

"What?" Shane says and I open my eyes to find him staring

at me. "You spent six weeks in his bed and he never tasted your pussy?"

Jason grumbles in the background, but I try and tune him out and focus on Shane. "No. He was more into receiving than giving."

Shane shakes his head and stares at Jason. "You are the biggest fucktard I have ever met in my life. Do you still fuck women without eating pussy? You must be a real hit with the ladies."

"Fuck you, man. We were just kids back then," Jason protests.

"He older than you?" Shane frowns at me.

"Yeah. He was twenty. His parents paid for his apartment and car," I reply, my cheeks still pink.

"Twenty? You weren't a kid, asshole, and even if you were... Fuck, I've been eating pussy since I was fifteen."

A sharp stab of jealousy pierces my chest. "Hey!" I nudge him in the ribs.

Realizing what he just said, he smiles at me and gives me a soft kiss on the forehead. "I have never enjoyed eating any as much as yours, Jessie, nor have I partaken so frequently as I do with you."

"You're such a poet," I say with a sigh, making him smile wider. His hand slides beneath my dress again, and for a moment there is only me and him in the room as he drags his pointer finger through my wet folds before circling my swollen clit. "Ah," I whimper, clinging to his neck.

"What the fuck?" Jason hisses, struggling in his bindings and reminding me he's there.

"Did he ever make you come, sweetheart?" Shane growls as he goes on rubbing the sensitive bud of flesh.

"No," I breathe.

"Yes I fucking did," Jason snarls.

"My girl said you didn't," Shane laughs softly.

"She's fucking lying," Jason insists. His bruised ego clearly winning out over his survival instinct because Shane's face turns dark with anger.

"Did you just call my wife a fucking liar?" he snarls.

"She's not gonna tell you I made her come, is she?" he goes on, digging himself deeper into a hole.

"Pretty sure she would, asshole," Shane snaps. "Because she doesn't fucking lie to me."

I curl my hand around his neck and press my cheek against his chest. That means so much to me given our incredibly shaky start when I had to hide who I really was from him and his brothers. Shane hates lying above anything else and it took him a long time to forgive me and to trust me again.

Jason grunts and grumbles in response.

"I tell you what, asshole," Shane says as he slides two fingers deep inside me, making me gasp as I coat him in a rush of slick heat. "I'll make my girl come right now, and you can hear what her actual orgasms sound like, rather than the ones she faked for you just to get you to leave her the fuck alone? How's that?" He spits out the last words — laced with anger and rage.

I feel it coursing through him but despite that, his fingers are gentle inside me, as though he's purposely holding back all of the emotion that is trying to spill out.

"Shane," I whimper as he brings me close to the edge.

He brushes the pad of his thumb over my clit and presses his mouth against my ear. "I know, sweetheart. I got you."

"I c-can't," I bury my head against his shoulder. "Not in front of him."

"You want me to stop?"

"No," I rock my hips against his hand. "I just can't let go."

"You can. Just focus on me, Jessie," he whispers as he works his fingers deeper, pressing against my G-spot and making my entire body tremble.

I breathe in the scent of him, inhaling his familiar cologne and that something else that I can never put my finger on, but which is just so uniquely him. I rub my cheek against his hard chest, taking comfort in its firm, reassuring warmth. His hand flexes on my waist, reminding me that he is holding onto me tight — that he's got me and that I have nothing to fear when I'm in his arms.

I curl my fingers in his hair, winding a strand around my fingertip.

"Shane," I breathe as my walls pulse around his fingers.

"Show him how hard you come for me," he orders, loud enough for Jason to hear and in that deep, commanding tone that vibrates through my bones and seems to be hardwired to my brain.

My body responds on instinct and my climax washes over me in a deep, bone shuddering, wave.

"Good girl," he whispers before he kisses the top of my head, massaging his fingers inside me until he has wrung out every last drop. "You hear that, dipshit? That's how to make my girl come," he says to Jason.

"Fuck you," Jason hisses.

"Is that the only comeback in your repertoire?" Shane laughs darkly, his fingers still inside me as he taunts his captive audience.

"Now if I thought you were worthy of such a show, I would spread my wife out on this desk and eat her pussy. Show you how to really make her scream," he says as he slides his fingers out of me, sucking them clean again before he goes on. "From the bulge in your jeans, I'd say you'd enjoy that a whole lot. But you're not fit to see her like that — not even close."

"You're sick," Jason spits.

CHAPTER THREE

"I'm sick? Says the man tied to chair with a raging boner,"
Shane laughs harder. Then he fixes my skirt and takes my hand,
pulling me into a standing position. "Go to the restroom, sweetheart. Get yourself cleaned up while I have a word with Jason
here."

I look back at Jason for the first time since Shane had me sit
on the desk. He's red in the face. He struggles against his bonds.
He's an asshole, yes. But he looks kind of pathetic sitting there
like that.

I place a hand on Shane's cheek and he presses his face into
my palm. "Don't kill him."

He glares at me. His jaw twitching as he maintains his
temper a little while longer. I'm pretty sure Jason is going to
bear the brunt of his wrath as soon as I walk into the restroom.
"I won't," he eventually agrees. "For you."

"No, not for me," I push onto my tiptoes and brush my lips
over his. "For you. Because he is not worth the blood on your
hands."

Shane Ryan might be one of the most ruthless men I know,
but I also know that it always costs him to take someone's life.
No matter how easily and skillfully he appears to do it.

"I love you," he breathes out the words as though it pains
him to say them.

"I know," I reply with a smile. That's usually our standard
reply when the other one says I love you. It all started because
he used to be an arrogant asshole, but now it's kind of our
thing.

He grabs my elbow, pulling me closer until our bodies are
pressed tightly together. "No. Not tonight, Jessie. Say the
words."

I blink at him. Is he feeling insecure? Shane Ryan? I stare
into his dark green eyes. "I love you, Shane. We were written in
the stars."

That makes a smile flicker over his face before he pulls my face closer and kisses me. Hard. His teeth clash against mine as his tongue claims my mouth. I melt against him as he pours some of the anger in his veins out into me instead. And I swallow it all gladly. Letting him take whatever he needs.

FOUR
SHANE

As soon as she is in the restroom, I walk over to the piece of shit sitting tied to a chair in the corner. I lean over him, my hands on the armrests.

"Why did you follow her in here?" I snarl.

"I thought I w-was helping her," he stammers.

"Helping her how?"

"You're kind of a controlling..." he doesn't finish the sentence.

"So what? You were going to rescue her from me? Is that it?"

"I thought she was scared of you," he says, avoiding my eyes. Useless sack of shit.

"I warned you I would break your hand if you touched her," I remind him.

"I know," he snivels. "But I never hurt her."

I press my face closer to his, anger burning in my chest. "No, because if you had you would be screaming in fucking agony right now. I would peel your skin from your body while you were still alive, you fuck!" I spit the words and he flinches at the venom in my tone. He has no idea who he's dealing with. On another night, I might show him, but I made her a promise. And she is all I want. Dealing with this waste of oxygen would only keep me from her.

I free his right hand from the cable binding him to the chair.

"W-what," he whimpers as I thread my thick fingers through his, pushing back until I hear the satisfying crunch of bone.

He screams so loudly that I have to punch him in the mouth to shut him up. He blinks up at me, blood running from his lip and tears in his eyes.

"If you ever come to my club again. If you ever go near her again. Speak to her. Touch her. Jerk off while you're thinking about her, I will find you and I will crush every bone in your body. Do you understand me?" I squeeze his broken fingers harder and his face twists in agony.

"Yes," he nods as tears run down his cheeks.

When I let his hand go, it drops limply to his side. I untie him quickly and pull him to his feet before opening the door and signaling one of my bouncers. "See this piece of shit out and never allow him in here again."

"Of course, boss," he says with a nod as he takes hold of Jason by his good arm and leads him through the club.

I'm leaning against the desk, hands shoved in my pockets as she walks out of the bathroom.

"Where is Jason?" she whispers.

"He left."

She makes her way toward me and places her hands on my chest. "Did he walk out of here or was he carried?"

I arch an eyebrow at her. "He walked."

She nods her head and smiles at me.

"You're not gonna though," I slide my hands to her waist, my fingertips gripping her tightly.

"I'm not?"

"No." Standing up, I spin her around so she's facing the desk. Pressing my lips against her ear, I inhale the smell of her — shampoo and the citrus perfume she wears. I could fucking eat her. "You won't be able to walk once I'm done with you."

My cock is aching for her. I press it against her backside, dragging her over my length.

"You think?" she breathes.

"I know. But don't worry. I'll carry you," I whisper in her ear as I start to unbuckle my belt. "Because your legs are gonna be shaking, sweetheart."

"Shane," my name leaves her lips on a breathy moan.

I pull her tiny mini skirt up over her ass before I push her down to lie face down on the desk. I love taking her like this. Driving myself into her and watching my shaft as it gets coated in her thick, creamy cum. Pulling my cock out of my pants, I nudge her legs further apart with my knee and line myself up at her entrance.

"You make me so fucking hard, Jessie." She wiggles her ass, trying to make me slide inside her but I hold back. "I've had this all damn night, sweetheart. You have any idea how uncomfortable this has been?"

"No," she giggles.

I slap her ass hard, making her suck in a breath. I glance down at the red mark on her perfect cream skin and it makes me smile. She is mine.

"Shane, please," she whimpers and my cock throbs.

I love how much she loves a spanking. How much she loves my hands on her. The way her body responds to every single touch.

Sliding myself deep into her, I moan even louder than she

does at the relief of being inside her. Her silky heat swallowing my cock and squeezing me in her tight channel. There is no better feeling in this world than being buried in her.

I grab onto her hips and drive deeper, making her cry out.

"You wore this tiny skirt to drive me crazy all night, didn't you, sweetheart?" I growl as I rail into her. "Because you knew I would fuck you like this as soon as I could get my hands on you."

"No," she whimpers. "It was..." she trails off, groaning loudly as I slam into her even harder.

"You feel how hard you make me? I can't get enough of you, Jessie," I groan as my balls tighten and heat pools at the base of my spine.

"Shane!"

"Who do you belong to, sweetheart?"

"You," she pants as her walls tighten around me and I feel her orgasm cresting.

"Say it louder," I grunt, fucking her harder than she deserves, but I'm feral for her. The thought of that prick's hands on her, of all of the jackasses in here tonight who looked at her and thought that they might have a shot, it makes the rage burn inside me. I am a possessive asshole when it comes to her and I know it. I allow people to look at her, to want her, to want to taste and touch what is mine. Because the knowledge that she belongs to me and they will never have her makes me feel invincible.

She makes me invincible.

"You," she screams as her climax rips through her, making her hot little pussy squeeze my dick, wrenching my own orgasm from me as she milks me.

I lean over her, my lips pressed against her ear. "Damn fucking right you do," I hiss as I empty myself into her.

When I'm done, I tuck my cock back into my pants, pull

down her skirt and scoop her into my arms, holding her still trembling body close to my chest.

She snakes an arm around my neck, her warm fingers curling a strand of my hair.

"I love you," she whispers as she nestles her head against my chest and I carry her out of the office and through the club.

It's not as crowded as it was an hour ago, but it's still busy enough for us to draw attention as I walk through to the exit that leads to the basement at the back of the club. It consists of two doors. One has a passcode and the other can only be accessed by our fingerprints.

I notice the concern in some of the faces as we pass by, and I hold her closer, not wanting any drunken hands to touch her to check if she's okay. I mean if they asked me, I'd happily tell them she can't walk because I just fucked her brains out.

She buries her face in my neck, her breath hot on my skin.

"Almost home, sweetheart."

"Hmm," she murmurs contentedly.

A FEW MOMENTS LATER, I step out of the elevator that leads to our penthouse apartment. Conor is standing in the hallway waiting for us, his hands stuffed into the pockets of his sweatpants.

"You see all that?" I ask him.

He can watch the feed from the security cameras in the club from up here, and he also has cameras in his office. And he is always watching her.

"Yeah," he grinds out the word, his jaw clenched tightly shut.

Jessie lifts her head and blinks at him. I feel the tension creeping into her body as she stiffens in my arms. She thinks he's pissed at her, but I know him better than that.

He walks over to us. "Give her to me."

I kiss her head softly before I allow him to take her from my arms.

"Are you, okay, angel?" he asks, running his hand over her hair as he squeezes her tight. He turns and starts to walk down the hallway to our bedroom and I fall into step beside him.

"Yes. And I can walk if you like?"

"I don't like," he snaps.

"Are you mad?" she whispers.

"Not at you," he replies, giving me the side eye.

"Please don't be mad at Shane. I don't want you to fight," she says, placing her hand on his face.

"We won't fight, angel. Promise," he reassures her before kissing her forehead.

Liar!

"Good." Jessie yawns. "Are we all going to bed?"

"Soon. I just need to talk to Shane first. Mikey and Liam are waiting for you."

"You said you wouldn't fight," she reminds him.

"We won't," I tell her. I have no intention of fighting with him over this.

"You sure you're okay?" he asks her again and the simmering anger bristles beneath my skin.

Of course she's okay. She was with me. Like I would let anyone hurt her. But I don't say any of those things right now because I don't want to argue in front of her.

He carries her to bed where Liam is lying awake waiting for her.

"Hey, baby," our younger brother says with a smile, seemingly unaware of what took place downstairs.

"Hey," she says as Conor sets her on her feet.

"Get in here, Red," Mikey grumbles, half asleep.

"I just need to freshen up first," she whispers

I want to tell her no. I want my cum running out of her while she lies between my brothers, but maybe it's not me she's washing away? So, I remain silent.

She looks between Conor and me, worry etched on her beautiful face.

"I just want to talk to him," Conor says quietly.

She narrows her eyes at us. "Okay," she finally says with a sigh. "But you'll come to bed soon, right?"

I place my hand on her waist and drop a soft kiss on the top of her head. "Very soon, sweetheart."

"Yeah," Conor agrees and together we watch her walk to the bathroom, her hips and ass swaying seductively in that skintight skirt.

Only when she's disappeared from view do Conor and I walk out of the room.

"What the fuck, Shane?" he snarls as soon as we're out in the hallway.

"He didn't see anything."

"He saw her come. He heard her," he snaps, his brow furrowed in anger.

"It's no worse than what you did in front of Gia. In fact it's less so."

He spins on his heel, glaring at me. "I did that for her. Because she needed me to. What you just did..." he scrubs a hand over his beard. "That was only for you."

I glare back at him. The rage is still bubbling inside me, just beneath the surface. Even fucking her didn't get it out of me. I should have killed him. I should have worked out every bit of anger and jealousy on him. He touched her.

He said...

Fuck! Conor is right.

"I know," I admit and he blinks at me in surprise. I doubt he was expecting that admission so easily. "He said she was scared of me, Con. He said he was protecting her from me."

"Jessie?" he frowns. "Scared of you?"

"That's what he said." I swallow hard.

"But you know she's not."

"Yeah, I do. But, I dunno, Con," I shake my head. "I needed him to know it. I needed him to see how much she trusts me. I would have fucked her too, but I knew you'd be watching."

"Fuck," Conor says with a sigh, his anger at me seeping out of him as his shoulders drop. "Who the fuck was he?"

"Some guy she met when she was eighteen."

My younger brother listens intently as I tell him everything Jessie told me about Jason Donegan.

"You should have killed him," he snarls.

"I know," I admit.

"She asked you not to?" he says with a faint smile.

"Yup."

"Simp," he laughs and shakes his head. But he would have done exactly the same and we both know it.

"Besides, I half expected you to come down there and kill him yourself."

"You seemed to have it handled," he says with a shrug.

I smile at his trust in me. He never undermines me even when he doesn't agree with my methods. He backs me one hundred percent and then argues with me about it later. Just the two of us. It's the way it's always been.

"You want a nightcap or shall we just go to bed?" I ask, looking at the door a few feet away from us where she and our younger brothers are sleeping. I'm still on edge and I won't be able to sleep yet.

"Whiskey or Jessie?" he says, sucking on his top lip as though he's deep in thought.

I think about which of those two things is going to make me

feel better about what happened tonight. There is only one answer. She's the answer to everything. "Bed then?"

He nods his head and puts an arm around my shoulder and we head back to the bedroom.

CHAPTER
FIVE

JESSIE

Three days before Christmas

I press a soft kiss on Finn's cheek as he sits contentedly in Mikey's arms sucking on a chunk of pineapple, before bending and scooping Ella up for a cuddle. She grabs my hair and pulls with an excitable squeal before wriggling to get back down to the floor where she can continue crawling around and causing mayhem. I place her back down and she gives me a beautiful smile in return.

"Our little girl is gonna turn us all gray by the time we're thirty, Red," Mikey whispers.

I crouch down on my heels and take Liam's sneaker from her, just before she sticks it into her mouth. "She is not!" I insist. "She's just spirited, aren't you, baby girl?"

"Spirited? That's what we used to call Mikey, and look how that worked out," Conor laughs as he comes up behind me, picking Ella up from the floor again. She doesn't resist him though. She giggles as he hoists her high up into the air. Such a Daddy's girl.

"She's gonna be a warrior princess, aren't you, baby?" Conor says and she squeals in delight.

Meanwhile, her twin brother looks on, happily eating his pineapple. They have such different temperaments.

Conor tucks Ella into the crook of his arm and gives Finn a kiss on the head too before he focuses on me.

"Where are you going?" he says, looking me up and down. I usually don't wear shoes, or many clothes in the apartment, but I am bundled up ready to brave the New York winter.

"Going to collect my dress for tomorrow night from Callie," I say with a grin.

I am so excited to see it and even more excited to wear it tomorrow night for the masked ball. Callie owns a boutique in Manhattan and she is an artist when it comes to clothes. She knows what suits me and my coloring way better than I do.

"I'll come with you," Conor says with a wicked glint in his eye. No doubt remembering the very first time he and I had sex in Callie's dressing room — and the many times since.

"No you won't," Liam says as he walks into the room wearing only one sneaker. "I'm taking Jessie shopping."

"But taking her shopping is kind of my thing," Conor says with a frown.

"I've been looking for that," Liam says, spying his stray sneaker on the floor.

"The pint sized terror stole it," Mikey says, indicating Ella, who has started to wriggle now that she doesn't have Conor's full attention.

"Sorry, bro. I haven't spent any time alone with my wife for three days," Liam says as he pulls on his shoe. "I get the shopping trip."

"Fuck!" Conor mutters just as Ella starts to cry and hold out her arms to me.

"Oh, you want your mama when you're upset," I chuckle as I take her from Conor and give her a quick squeeze before placing her back on the floor where she wants to be.

"Besides, we have to go to The Peacock Club after to make sure everything's set up for tomorrow," Liam adds as he stands up straight.

The Peacock Club is one of a string of exclusive, private clubs we own across the States and Europe. They are sex clubs which cater to every kink imaginable. Every year they hold a Christmas Eve masked ball and they are the hottest tickets in the city. We didn't go last year because I was eight months pregnant, and I had thought we wouldn't make this years either. None of us wanted to miss our children's first Christmas Eve, but Shane insisted that they move the ball to the day before – a Christmas Eve, Eve masked ball – so now we are all going.

Liam, Mikey and I mostly look after The Peacock Clubs, while Conor handles the main nightclub, The Emerald Shamrock, which makes up half the basement and the entire first floor of our building.

"I can come with you to the club," Mikey says with a flash of his eyebrows, never one to miss out on an opportunity to visit and make use of one of the basement rooms while we're there.

"No. They're going to work, you fucking deviant. Besides, you're watching the babies," Conor reminds him. "I have some work to do."

"Why can't you watch the babies and let me have an afternoon of fun with my wife too?" Mikey suggests with a wicked grin.

"Because I have to work."

"But you were going to take the afternoon off to go shopping with Jessie?" Mikey reminds him.

"Yeah, well shopping with Jessie is worth taking an afternoon off for."

"But looking after our beautiful children isn't?" Mikey teases.

"Of course that would be worth it if they didn't have a perfectly good father right here already."

"You think I'm a good father?" Mikey pretends to choke up and wipes a fake tear from his eye.

"You're an asshole," Conor says with a roll of his eyes.

"Shall we go, baby?" Liam cuts through their bantering and slides an arm around my waist.

"Yes," I say with a smile.

"Will you buy some new panties please? Just for me?" Mikey asks me with a wink.

"Of course," I reply giving him a quick kiss.

"And get something for me, angel," Conor growls as he comes up beside me, pressing his lips against my ear. "Something you don't mind me tearing in half later."

LIAM SITS IN THE PLUSH, purple velvet chair in the dressing room of Callie's boutique. His legs sprawled and his hand resting on his chin as he watches me intently.

"I picked everything you asked for, Jessie," Callie says with a smile as her eyes sweep the room and land on a pile of underwear. "And also Conor called me a half hour ago and added to the list," she adds with a soft giggle.

"I bet he did," I laugh too.

She places a soft, manicured hand on my arm and sucks in a deep breath as though she's holding in her excitement. "But first, your gown," she squeaks, clapping her hands together. "Shall we try it?"

"Yes," I give a little squeal of excitement too. I am so pumped for the ball and Callie has promised to find me the perfect gown.

"It's behind here," she says, pulling back the thick velvet curtain a little and ushering me to step inside.

"Um, I thought you tried on clothes out here, baby?" Liam says.

I turn and smile at him. "I do, but not my gown."

"No," Callie agrees, shaking her head at him.

His brows knit into a frown. "Why?"

"Because you're not allowed to see it until the ball," I admonish him.

"So fucking unfair," he grumbles.

"Your Jessie has plenty of beautiful clothes to try on for you after her gown," Callie tells him with a wink.

AFTER I TRY on my gown, which is exquisitely perfect, Callie zips it into a bag and hangs it for me. When we're done, I step out of the small curtained area in just my underwear. She bustles around beside me, sorting clothes into piles. Liam, however, simply stares at me, his dark eyes roaming over my body and making me blush.

"Would you like me to stay and help?" Callie asks as she stands straight, blowing a stray curl from her forehead.

"No," Liam says immediately, making her laugh.

"He is so like his brother, no?" she says to me with a pop of one perfectly manicured eyebrow.

"He is," I agree.

"You both have one hour before the store opens again," she adds with a smile before she slips out of the room, leaving us alone.

"So now you try on all of these?" Liam asks, his eyes narrowed as he glances around the room.

"If you'd like me to?" I offer. I have no doubt that all of it will fit me perfectly because Callie knows my size and what suits me. "Where should I start?"

His Adam's apple bobs in his throat as he swallows hard. "The workout gear," he says with a low growl.

I smile as I walk over to it. His tastes are so different to his brothers. Conor would have gone straight for the black mini dress, while Mikey and Shane would have chosen the sexy underwear.

Fingering the soft, lilac material I flutter my eyelashes at him. "You know I don't usually wear underwear with my workout gear?"

"Yeah," he grunts.

"Okay," I whisper as I unhook my bra, keeping my gaze fixed on his as I peel it off and over my arms.

His eyes darken and he licks his lips.

Dropping my bra to the floor, I slide my hands over my stomach and hips, hooking my thumbs into the band of my panties before slowly working them down my legs.

"Fuck, Jessie," he groans as he pushes himself out of the chair. In a few swift moves he has me wrapped in his huge arms, my back against his chest and his face in my hair. "You know what you do to me, baby," he growls in my ear.

"I thought you wanted me to try on the clothes?" I whisper, aware that I won't be doing any such thing now, and that's fine with me.

"Is there any chance Callie will come back in here?"

"No. She knows not to disturb us."

"Fuck!" he hisses.

Unlike Shane and Mikey, he prefers privacy. Even the

thought of someone other than his brothers hearing us, would bother him.

"Does Conor fuck you in here?" he asks as he starts to unzip his jeans, keeping his other arm wrapped tightly around me.

"Yes."

He sucks in a deep breath and I feel him pumping his cock behind me before he picks me up with one arm and carries me across the small room until we're standing in front of the full length mirror. I drop my eyes instinctively and he grabs my jaw, tilting my head up so that I'm looking at our reflection. "Look how fucking beautiful you are, baby."

I look at him instead, staring into his eyes in the mirror.

"I said look at you, not me."

"I'd rather look at you," I whisper.

His lips dust over my ear. "Then watch me, baby. Watch my hands worship you."

I look at his hand gripping my jaw and follow it as he rubs it down my neck, onto my chest before he squeezes one of my breasts, making me moan softly. Then the other slides from my waist where he's holding me, gliding over my stomach. Over the gentle roundness in my lower abdomen that I can't seem to flatten no matter how hard I work out.

I close my eyes as his fingertips trace over the silvery stretch-marks I have now.

"Open your eyes, Jessie," he orders.

"You're so bossy," I protest as my eyes flicker open and I look at his huge hands on my stomach and breasts. Who am I kidding though? I love bossy Liam.

"Yeah?" he says, his warm breath on my neck making me shiver. "And you are even more beautiful now than you ever were. You gonna grow some more of my babies in here?" he growls, splaying his fingers across my abdomen.

"Hmm," I murmur as his fingers slide lower.

"Spread those legs for me, baby."

I do as he asks me, allowing him to slide his hand between my thighs. He cups my pussy as he tugs on my nipples with his other hand and wet heat pools in my center.

"Who was the first out of us to kiss you?"

"You were," I breathe, remembering the night on the sofa with him and Mikey. It feels like just yesterday but also a lifetime ago.

"And who was the first one of us to taste this beautiful pussy?"

"You," I gasp as he starts to circle my clit with the tip of his pointer finger.

"You've always been mine, Jessie," he squeezes possessively.

"You were the first man I ever kissed for real," I remind him.

He brushes his lips over the sensitive skin on my neck. "I know, baby. And now, I want you to watch yourself while you fall apart for me. And then you're gonna watch me fuck you. You think you can keep quiet while I do that?"

"I'll try," I promise.

"You'd better do more than try, baby. Nobody else gets to hear you come but me, okay?" He slides a finger inside me while he goes on squeezing and tugging my nipples and I have to bite on my lip to stop myself from crying out as a wave of pleasure rolls through me. I moan softly instead.

"Good girl," he whispers as he rubs the knuckle of his thumb over my clit while he adds a second finger.

"Liam," I whimper. "You feel so good."

"You too, baby. Your pussy is dripping for me. I can't wait to slide my cock inside you too."

Dear God. His filthy talk really isn't helping me be quiet.

"Please?" I beg, pressing my hands flat against the mirror as my legs tremble. "I want you inside me."

"I am inside you, baby," he chuckles as he drives his fingers deeper. "Don't you feel that?"

"Ah," I groan as wet heat slicks his fingers.

"Yeah you do," he growls and the sound vibrates through my body. "You were made for me, weren't you?"

"Yes," I whimper as he massages my inner walls and rubs my clit while he rolls my sensitive nipple between his finger and thumb.

"Fuck, Liam!" I hiss as quietly as I can as the first waves of my orgasm pulse through my core.

"Look how beautiful you are when you come for me," he growls as he works his fingers expertly.

I look at myself in the mirror. My skin flushed pink. My body cradled in his strong hands. This is the body that he loves. The one that his brothers love. It is an irrefutable fact. One that I know in my bones.

His huge frame almost dwarfs me. His powerful thighs either side of mine. His thick biceps cocooning me — full of warmth and strength. He is strong and I am soft.

But my body is strong too. I grew two babies. Two incredible tiny humans who are going to change the world.

"I love you," I breathe as my climax bursts through me, coating his fingers as he wrings the last drops with his skilled hands.

"Love you too, baby," he whispers in my ear, sliding his fingers out of me. "Now lean forward and spread a little wider for me."

I widen my stance, dropping my head between my shoulders slightly as he grabs hold of my hip with one hand and his cock with the other. He presses the crown against my opening and I draw in a deep breath. I still want more of him. I always want more.

"Keep your eyes in the mirror. Watch how I fuck you."

I look in the mirror, my eyes on him rather than myself and watch his almost roll back in his head as he drives his cock into me.

"Fuck. You feel so good," he growls. "So. Fucking. Good." He thrusts on every word, rocking me forward onto my tiptoes every time he does and hitting me at the perfect angle.

Over and over again he rails into me. His eyes never leave my body as he fucks me relentlessly.

"Liam," I pant, my breath fogging the glass.

"Come for me again, baby. Squeeze my cock with your tight pussy so I can I fill you with my cum."

Oh sweet Jesus!

"Oh, God!" I shout out and he clamps a hand over my mouth, pulling me back so that my back is flush against his chest again.

"I warned you to keep quiet," he groans in my ear.

Lifting me from the floor, he carries me to the huge purple chair and drops me onto my knees on the seat. Pressing a hand between my shoulder blades, he pushes me forward so my face is pressing against the back cushion.

"Bite down, baby. Because I'm giving you another one of them."

"Liam, I can't," I whimper. "If you make me come again, I might ruin this chair."

"You won't," he soothes, holding my hips in place as he slides deep inside me. "Just let me fuck you."

"If you make me squirt all over this beautiful chair..." I trail off because he starts to trail kisses over my shoulders as he reaches in front of me and starts to rub my clit.

I squeeze my eyes tightly shut as my third orgasm crests and my entire body starts to shudder. Stars flicker behind my eyelids as he maintains his relentless fucking and rubbing and kissing. I'm so sensitive. I'm going to pass out or...

"Liam," I whimper again.

"I said bite down," he reminds me.

I press my face into the deep velvet cushion, muffling my moans as I come.

Hard.

I soak his jeans and the cushion I'm kneeling on while Liam sucks on my neck as he grinds deeper into me, filling me with his own release.

When he finally stops, he pants in my ear and I look down at the mess we've made. The chair is soaked in my cum.

"I told you we'd ruin the chair. Callie is going to kill us."

"I'll buy her a new one," he chuckles as he peppers soft kisses over my back, making me squirm.

"She's going to know what we were doing in here," I tell him, even though I'm pretty sure she already does.

He looks down too. "Fuck," he mumbles. "I'll tell her I spilled a drink."

"What drink would that be, Einstein?" I ask with a roll of my eyes.

He slaps my ass. "Don't be cheeky," he growls and I giggle.

He pushes himself up and zips up his jeans.

"You're in so much trouble, Liam Ryan. If Callie bans us from her boutique, Conor is going to be so pissed at you."

That makes him falter and he screws his eyes closed. "We'll take the cushion and I'll have someone come pick up the rest of it and deliver a new one by the end of the day."

"Why are we taking the cushion?" I turn and frown in confusion. "Maybe we could just flip it to the dry side?"

He shakes his head. "No. It's soaked in your cum, baby. It's coming with us."

"You're serious?" I ask as I search for my discarded underwear.

He hands me my panties. "Deadly."

Taking them from his outstretched hand, I arch an eyebrow at him. "You happen to know a guy who sells giant purple velvet chairs then?"

Pinching the bridge of his nose, he sighs deeply before he says, "I'll get something else for today. Just get dressed so we can plan our escape."

I laugh, wondering how he's going to explain his way out of this. Once I'm dressed, Liam calls Callie into the room. He's flipped the cushion so the huge wet patch can't be seen. His jeans are also wet but he hides that with his coat.

"We'll take all of the clothes," he says. "And the chair."

"The chair?" Callie blinks at him in confusion.

"Yup. It's going to be Conor's Christmas present."

"You can't have my chair," Callie laughs softly.

"I'm gonna need it," Liam replies. "I'll have a replacement one sent within the hour and then if you let me know where to get the purple one from, I'll have it here as soon as possible."

"But that's not possible. It was custom made. The designer doesn't make them any longer. It cost me fifteen thousand dollars."

"I'll give you fifty thousand for it," Liam offers and I suppress a grin. That chair is from a chain store and they still sell them now.

"But it was a family heirloom," she adds.

Liam frowns at her. "But you just said..."

Callie and I burst out laughing at the same time and Liam shakes his head.

"You can take the chair. But yes I want a new one. Jessie knows where to buy them," Callie says with a giggle as she wanders out of the room.

Liam turns and trains his gaze on me. "You know where to buy them?"

I chew on my lip, trying to look sweet and adorable. "Yeah," I whisper.

He crosses the room in two strides, pulling me into his arms. "If I was into spanking..." he breathes, brushing my hair behind my ear. "Your pretty ass would be red by the time we left here."

"You've spanked me plenty of times," I remind him.

"A slap on the ass is not a spanking, baby," he growls, making a shiver skitter along my spine.

"I would love a spanking from you."

He narrows his eyes at me. "Haven't you had enough fun for one afternoon?"

"Not nearly enough," I whisper and he laughs softly.

CHAPTER
SIX
JESSIE

Two days before Christmas

I adjust my green and gold mask and take a deep breath as I grip the door handle. Looking down at the deep emerald green material of my dress, I blink back an unexpected tear. I have never been to a ball before. I've never worn a dress as exquisite as this one. Even my wedding dress was simple. This is made of the softest velvet I have ever felt — softer than a baby's skin. It's strapless and studded with Swarovski crystals all along the split up my thigh, which is so high it's almost indecent. They sparkle every time I move.

I feel like a princess.

I can't even imagine what it cost because Callie wouldn't tell me and my husbands insisted on paying for it. I hope they love it as much as I do.

I walk out of the bedroom and the four of them are standing in the hallway in their matching tuxedos waiting for me. It's a good thing I'm not wearing panties because they would have just burst into flames.

"Fuck, baby," Liam says with a low whistle.

"That dress is hot, Red," Mikey says as he walks straight over to me and slides his hands around my waist.

"You look beautiful, Mrs. Ryan," Chester says and I realize I hadn't even noticed him standing in the hallway too. I was too mesmerized by the four hot devils in the finest suits I have ever seen.

Chester is the brother's longest serving and most trusted employee, and along with his wife, Rosie, he is our babysitter for the evening. There is also a team of four ex Navy SEALS in the basement making sure that nobody can get to the apartment.

"What did you say?" Conor growls as he glares at Chester.

"Relax, Con," Shane laughs. "She's pretty hard not to look at."

"I'll just go check on the twins," Chester mumbles apologetically.

"Thank you," I say to him with a smile.

"Call us for anything at all," Conor reminds him as he walks down the hallway.

"Will do, Boss," he calls back. "Have a great time."

Conor watches after him. It took us a long time to trust anyone with our children's safety, but Chester and his wife are almost part of the family now, and his small unit of security do an amazing job.

When there is just the five of us in the hallway, Conor, Shane and Liam walk toward me until I'm standing in the middle of all four of them.

Conor looks down at the split in my dress, his dark eyes twinkling. But it's Shane who slides his hand inside and brushes his fingers over my bare pussy.

"She wearing panties?" Conor asks him.

"Nope," Shane grins. "Freshly shaved too."

I blush and Conor closes his eyes. "Dammit, angel," he hisses.

"I can't really wear underwear with this dress," I protest. "It's so tight."

"Fits you like a second skin, Red," Mikey says appreciatively as he runs his hands over my ass.

"Can we just stay home?" Liam groans as he trails his lips over my bare shoulder.

"No," I say, but his brothers laugh.

"We have a room booked too," Shane reminds him.

Mikey rubs a hand over his beard. "And now that Conor has given the green light for public-"

"It's not a green light," Conor snarls.

"But some public fuckery must be permissible after what you did, bro?" Mikey winks at him. "And I mean, we all came prepared, right?"

"Prepared?" I blink at him.

He pulls his pocket square out and reveals it's actually a large white handkerchief. "For any spillages," he says with a wicked grin.

I look at the three of them and they all nod to confirm they too have white handkerchiefs.

"Can't have you spoiling that beautiful dress, sweetheart," Shane whispers.

"Maybe I should wear panties too?" I suggest, wondering if I'm going to able to sit down at all tonight without staining this dress.

"No," Mikey and Liam reply.

"We need to leave," Shane says, checking his watch.

"Wait. Where are your masks?" I ask.

"We've got them," Liam says, patting his breast pocket. "We'll put them on outside the club."

"Let's go before I tie you to my bed instead, angel," Conor says with a sigh, placing his hand on the small of my back and guiding me to the elevator.

MIKEY POURS CHAMPAGNE as we sit in the back of the limo. I sit on Liam's lap. I rarely get my own seat but that's fine with me because I'd much prefer to have one of them holding onto me.

"Just a small one for me, please. You know I get giddy when I drink bubbles."

"Yeah, and you're kinda giddy enough already, Red," Mikey says with a grin as he hands me my glass.

"I can't help it. It's Christmas. We're going to a masked ball. All of us at The Peacock Club," I shiver in anticipation.

"You need me to help you relax, baby?" Liam whispers in my ear, making goosebumps prickle over my forearms.

"How is that not gonna make her even more excited?" Conor asks his younger brother with a frown, but Liam's hand is already trailing up the inside of my thigh through the split in my dress.

"But she looks so damn good in this dress," Liam groans as he trails kisses over my throat.

Conor sighs but it's Shane's voice that stops Liam's fingers as they are just millimeters from my pussy. "If you make our girl come now and she starts moaning in this car, then someone is gonna fuck her. And if one of us fucks her..."

"We'll all want to fuck her," Conor finishes for him.

"And then we never get to the club," Mikey adds.

"Jessie's call," Shane says. "You want to go to the ball or you want to drive around the city all night being nailed in this car?"

I swallow. I mean on any other night the car option sounds good too. "I want to go to the ball," I whisper.

"Then your wish is my command, Cinderella," Liam says with a wink as he slides his hand from inside my dress.

Conor takes my hand and lifts it to his lips, brushing them over my fingertips while Liam dusts his lips over my ear. "Besides, we got all night, baby."

We do. A whole night with them in the club. With the use of a private room in the basement. My insides turn to molten lava at the thought.

It's going to be perfect.

CHAPTER
SEVEN

JESSIE

I actually gasp out loud when we walk into the club. Our manager, Evelyn, has done an incredible job with the place. At first glance it is decorated with elegantly tasteful Christmas garlands and ornaments, but on closer inspection, most of them have some kind of cock, pussy or something kinky on them. It is perfect for a masked Christmas Eve, Eve ball in a sex club.

I look at Liam who holds onto my hand. "It's perfect, isn't it?"

He nods his agreement.

"We should go find Evelyn and tell her."

Shane slides a hand onto my ass and whispers in my ear. "You can do that tomorrow, Mrs. Ryan. Tonight there will be no shop talk. We're just regular customers here."

I smile at him. I love that idea. And being here with four guys isn't that unusual for this place. Anything and everything goes.

"If we're just regular customers then I would like to take my wife for a dance," Mikey says, taking my other hand and nodding toward the dance floor.

Just as he says that the opening beats of *Pony* come on and I roll my eyes. There is no way he didn't plan that to happen.

"Look out, Magic Mikey is in the house," Liam laughs softly.

"Come on, Red, dance with me?" he says, tugging my hand.

"Just dancing, right?" Conor says with a frown.

"Oh, bro, we are gonna do so much more than dance," Mikey winks at him before he pulls me off into the crowd and finds us a dark spot on the dance floor.

"You shouldn't push his buttons like that," I giggle as I wrap my arms around his neck.

"Oh, but Red," he whispers in my ear. "I can guarantee he's going to be over here within ten minutes and then you're gonna have both of us here finger fucking you in the middle of this club."

"Mikey," I gasp as he steps back and starts busting out his best moves. His hand slides over his stomach as he rocks his hips and I bite on my lip as I watch him. Damn, he is so fine.

When he notices I'm not dancing, he wraps his arms around my waist. "Dance with me, Jessie."

"I hate dancing on my own," I whisper. "I feel self-conscious."

He frowns at me. "But I'm right here with you."

"I know, I mean... I like dancing like this. With you," I say as my cheeks flush pink.

He raises his eyebrows at me. "You mean you like my hands on you at all times?"

"Yes," I laugh.

"Then consider it done," he growls as he rocks his hips against mine. "But know I'm gonna have a raging boner the whole time."

"Yeah?" I bite on my lip and press my lips to his ear. "Watching you bust out your Magic Mikey routine gives me a lady boner."

"Fuck!" he groans in my ear.

Then he's walking me backwards until we're tucked away in a corner. His hand slides into the split in my dress until his fingers glide over my pussy and I shiver at his touch.

"Remember when I made you come in The Shamrock, Red?" he groans, reminding me of an evening we spent in our other nightclub as he slips a finger between my folds.

"Yes," I hiss.

"And remember how mad we made Conor?" he chuckles.

"Yeah," I whimper, remembering the aftermath of that whole event.

"Well, he must have seen me sneaking off into a dark corner with you because he's on his way over here right now."

With his final word he slides a finger inside me and my walls tighten around him.

"Oh, fuck," I gasp as strong hands slide over my abdomen and a hard chest is pressed against my back.

"You're a fucking deviant, Mikey," Conor says gruffly.

"Never claimed to be anything else," he replies with a grin as he leans his face closer to his older brother. "But you should feel how wet she is, bro."

Conor grunts in response, stepping closer to me and pinning my body against Mikey's until I'm sandwiched between the two of them. Mikey looks down at me and gently pumps his finger in and out of me. "You okay, Red?"

"Uh-huh," I mumble as slick heat coats his fingers and warmth spreads through my thighs.

My body shudders and Conor's hard cock digs into my back. He's so rigid and tense. I feel it in his arms and chest, as though he's holding back from something — either he wants to punch his little brother in the face, or he wants to touch me too.

When his hand slides over my abdomen until he reaches the

split in my dress, I realize which temptation he was fighting. Pulling the soft fabric aside to allow his hand inside too, he brushes the pad of his middle finger over my clit and I whimper with need.

Mikey palms the back of my head and presses my mouth against his neck. "Stay right here. We got you," he whispers.

God do they got me. The two of them work their fingers in and on my pussy like they each know what the other is thinking. I moan into Mikey's neck as he pushes deeper and Conor presses harder. Then in the space of one single song they have me coming on their hands and shuddering between them.

"Good girl," Conor whispers in my ear.

"Such a good fucking girl, Red," Mikey adds as he brushes back my hair.

"How long do we have to stay up here before we can make use of that fucking room downstairs?" Conor growls as he slides his hand from my dress.

Mikey does the same, sucking his fingers clean in full view of the crowd.

Meanwhile Conor takes his handkerchief from his pocket. "Keep her covered," he barks to Mikey as his hand slips between my thighs again.

"As if I wouldn't," Mikey says with a scowl.

"I can go to the rest-" I start to say but Conor is already wiping the soft cotton between my folds.

"I don't want you spoiling your beautiful dress, angel," he whispers in my ear.

"Then thank you."

"But I hope you don't ever plan on wearing it again after tonight, because I'm going to fucking ruin it later," he adds.

I gasp out loud. "You can't. It's too expensive, and it's way too gorgeous to ruin."

"Not as gorgeous as you, Red," Mikey grins.

"And we're going to ruin you too," Conor growls, making my insides turn to Jell-o.

I blow out a shaky breath. "As hot as that sounds, we only just got here and we can't go to the room downstairs yet."

"Fuck!" Conor grumbles.

"Shane has reserved us a booth anyway. Pretty sure he just watched us make you come on this dance floor and will be wanting to push some more boundaries tonight," Mikey adds with a laugh.

An hour later, Shane, Liam and I are making our way back to the booth after I wanted to see the displays in the other rooms. As we pass the stairs to the basement, I stop them.

"I need the powder room," I say.

We just passed the customer restrooms and the line was enormous but there's a staff bathroom downstairs that I could use.

"Shane Ryan?" a guy with gray hair wearing a red and black mask comes up beside us and says.

All of my husbands are wearing masks too but they are pretty recognizable anyway. Shane clearly knows this man and likes him because he smiles.

"Alfred," he says as he shakes his hand.

"And Mikey?" the man I now know is Alfred says to Liam.

"Liam," he corrects him.

"Sorry. You look even more alike with a mask on," Alfred laughs.

"And this is my wife, Jessie," Shane introduces me and I smile too. But now I am busting to pee.

"I need to use the ladies' room," I say, excusing myself.

Shane frowns at me.

"I'll go with her," Liam says and we both say goodbye to Alfred and make our way downstairs to the basement.

"I can go to the restroom alone, you know?" I say to Liam, reminded of a similar conversation I had with Shane a few evenings before.

"I know, but it's more fun with me," he says with a wink.

As we reach the bottom of the stairs, there is some kind of commotion going on in one of the rooms because a woman runs out crying and a half naked man comes running after her and bumps straight into Liam.

"What the fuck?" Liam snarls as he pushes the man off him.

"Cassidy!" he shouts after the fleeing woman.

"Did you do something to her?" Liam snarls.

"No," the man scowls at him.

Oh my God, I'm going to pee.

The hallways starts to fill up with people who are either startled by what's going on or simply on their way down here to use one of the rooms. There is usually a bouncer at the top of the stairs but I imagine he may have gone running after the crying woman. I hope she's okay.

Damn. Now I really need to pee.

"Liam. I gotta go now. I'll be right back," I say as I head off to the bathroom.

"Jessie, wait."

"I'll be right back," I call, turning the corner as I head to the staff restroom and straight into a bearded man in a Santa mask.

"Jessie Heaton? Twice in one week? This must be fate, right?" the familiar voice sneers. "And lucky for you I have a room here."

Jason!

I shout for Liam but there is too much noise down here now. People are jostling through the hallway. Jason grabs my arm, opening the door to the nearest room which he has clearly just come out of and pushing me inside.

There are three other men in there and they all look up as he walks in. They all wear masks. The Grinch, an elf and a reindeer.

"Where are the girls? One is no good to us?" The Grinch barks.

"Oh, but this one is even better," Jason sneers as he takes off his Santa mask. "She's the one who did this." He holds up his hand which I now see is in a cast.

"I didn't do that," I say but he pushes me further into the room and I stumble forward in my heels.

"Shut up. Fucking whore!" he spits.

"But where are the girls we were supposed to be hooking up with?" the elf asks.

"Couldn't fucking find them. I think they stood us up," Jason says with a shrug.

"So what? We all take turns on her?" The Grinch asks with a sneer as he removes his mask too. He has a dark goatee too and his eyes are similar to Jason's.

"Exactly, bro," Jason says, confirming they are brothers.

"Take turns on me?" I spit. "Have you lost your tiny fucking minds?"

"Did she just..." The Grinch looks at his brother. "Who the fuck is this bitch?"

I stare at The Grinch. Clearly he thinks he is somebody special. He's dressed in a finely tailored suit. Expensive leather shoes. He wears a fancy watch too. From here it looks like an Omega. Jason's parents were very wealthy. I remember how much he used to go on about how rich his family were. He always thought he was somebody special too.

The other two men in the room are dressed pretty similarly. I imagine they all think they have the balls to do what they're about to. I also imagine they probably get away with crap like this all the time. But clearly they have no idea who I am.

"I told you. That whore who used to fuck me for a place to stay. The one that had her asshole, psycho husband make me watch him finger fuck her," Jason answers The Grinch's question.

"If her husband is a psycho is this the wisest move?" the elf asks.

"Like he could touch us," the Grinch replies with a smug grin.

"Are you really that stupid that you think he won't annihilate every single one of you?" I say with a shake of my head. "You don't think he's looking for me right now?"

The Grinch shrugs. "He can look all he wants, princess. He ain't gonna find you down here. These rooms are private and soundproof. Those doors are made of solid steel. There are no cameras. Nobody gets in without a special keycard."

"Yeah, I know asshole, because I-"

Before I can finish that sentence and possibly save their lives by telling them who I am so they can let me go, Jason grabs me by the throat.

"You call my brother an asshole. Do you know who he is? He has friends, bitch. Powerful fucking friends."

"I guarantee none of them are powerful enough to save you if you don't let me go," I croak and he squeezes tighter.

"Let you go? When we haven't even started yet. You're gonna pay me back for the other night, you fucking slut! You think you can humiliate me and get away with it?"

He pushes me backward, letting go of my throat as he does. "Humiliate you? How exactly did I do that?"

He holds up his bandaged hand. "This! Making me watch you and him..." he spits out the words.

"I believe it was my husband who did both of those things.

Why don't you take this up with him?" I snarl as I take a step closer to him. "Because you are a fucking coward, that's why. He humiliated you, but you want to take that out on me?"

He presses his face closer to mine. "No. He will feel what I'm going to do to you, you filthy fucking whore!" he hisses. "Every time he looks at you, he's going to know what I did. Know that we all fucked your pretty little holes." He pulls a flick knife from his pocket and flashes it in front of my eyes.

I don't flinch. I glare at him instead. "You lay one finger on me and he will kill you, Jason. And he won't do it quickly. He will make you scream for mercy."

He seems to find that funny and he throws his head back with laughter. "I think I can handle him."

"I really don't think you can," I spit. "You certainly couldn't the other night."

He glares at me again, his teeth bared like a rabid animal. "I'm not on my own now though, am I?" He nods toward his three friends. "You have no idea who you've been fucking with, whore!"

I glare back at him. I think he is the one who has no idea who he's dealing with, but I don't say that. I let him go on thinking he's a big man — it all buys me some time until one of my husbands gets in here.

"Stop calling me a whore," I say instead.

He drags the tip of the blade over the soft skin of my neck. Fear prickles along my spine but I stay rooted to the spot, determined not to show any fear to this stupid asshole. "But you are a whore, Jessie," he snarls. "You slept with me for a place to stay."

I narrow my eyes at him. "Kind of makes you a sick, twisted piece of shit then!"

"And I saw you up there in the club. Oh yeah, I saw you. I hoped we might get a chance to talk alone. Letting your husband's buddies slide a hand inside your dress. Does he know that they do that? Does he like to pass you around?"

My nostrils flare as I suck in a breath. "He does not *pass me around,* asshole. They are not his buddies, they're his brothers, and they're my husbands too."

That certainly gets his attention. "You can't have more than one husband. It's illegal."

"Pretty sure my husbands don't give a crap about the law, as you're about to find out to your detriment if you don't let me go right now."

"You got four husbands?" Jason's brother asks me.

"Yes," I snap.

His face turns whiter than Santa's beard as he realizes who I am. He looks back at Jason before slapping him across the back of the head. "You fucking stupid prick. You said this was just some chick who fucked you over."

"Sh-she is," Jason stammers as he frowns at his brother.

"You have any fucking idea who she's married to?" his brother asks as he runs a hand through his hair. "Fuck!" he mutters, pacing back and forth while Jason stares at him.

"Who?"

"The Ryans, you fucking reject!"

"Who the fuck are they?" Jason snarls.

His brother stops pacing and glares at him so hard it's a wonder he doesn't burst into flames. "Only the goddamn Irish." He slaps Jason again. "Fucking." Slap. "Mafia."

"W-what?" Jason stammers.

"Yeah, dipshit," I say. "So let me go right now and they might not cut off your balls and make you eat them while I watch."

"We can't let her go, man," the reindeer says. "We need to get her out of here. Like now."

Oh, fuck!

"No. You need to let me go and get yourselves out of here," I say. "Before they find you."

"So you can tell your husbands what we did and have them come looking for us?" Jason's brother scowls.

I fold my arms over my chest. "How the hell do you expect to get me out of here without them noticing?"

"We could knock her out. Pretend she's drunk," the elf suggests.

"You'll never get past the bouncers. You think they don't know me?"

Jason's brother looks at his two buddies. "Where was that fire escape?"

"End of the hallway," the reindeer replies.

"You take me out of here and they will come for you," my voice trembles but I tip my jaw in defiance. I have dealt with scarier and tougher men than these before. "That is an inescapable fact. But you let me go back upstairs and you at least have a chance."

"Shut her the fuck up," Jason's brother orders.

Jason makes a grab for me but I dodge him and knee him in the balls, causing him to drop to the floor.

"You shouldn't have done that. Dumb bitch!" His brother snarls as he wraps a thick, tattooed hand around my throat and his two buddies close in on me too.

He squeezes tightly, making my head spin. I claw at his arms and try to suck in a breath as I prepare to try and fight my way out of this. I would rather die than let them take me away from this club. Because if they do manage to get me out of here, they only have one option and they know it. They need to make me disappear.

"You *really* shouldn't have done that, asshole," Mikey's voice washes over me and I almost pass out with relief. His fingers curl around Jason's brother's wrist as it's wrapped around my throat, and he squeezes hard enough that I hear the crunch of bone. The elf jumps on Mikey's back but he shrugs him off as though he's made of air.

When the grip on my throat loosens, I stagger backward, stumbling against the wall and rubbing the reddened skin on my neck.

"One of them has a knife," I croak but Mikey already has Jason's brother on the floor. He stamps on his head and the sickening crunch of bone almost makes me retch.

My eyes flicker closed as blood thunders around my body and I sway on my feet, feeling like I'm about to faint. That's when I feel the two strong arms wrapped around me and I sink against his chest, seeking the comfort and warmth of him. The familiarity of his touch, his smell, his arms — they all soothe me.

"Liam," I murmur.

"I got you, baby," he says, stroking my hair as he holds me tight.

"Get her home. Now!" Shane's deep voice fills the room and I look up to see him and Conor running inside.

"Come on. Let's get you out of here," Liam whispers as he picks me up and cradles me to his chest.

"I'm sorry," I rasp, my throat raw.

"Don't, Jessie," Shane barks as he grabs Jason by the jaw and pushes him back against the wall. Then he starts to pummel his face with his fist and Jason screeches in agony. Meanwhile Conor grabs both the elf and the reindeer by the throat at the same time. He doesn't even look at me and that makes me want to cry.

I have ruined the whole night.

"I said get her out of here, Liam," Shane barks again and the harshness in his tone makes me bury my face in Liam's chest.

Before we leave the room, I take a final glance back at Conor and Shane and the scene is like something from an action movie.

Conor has the reindeer in a headlock while he kicks the elf in the chest, sending him flying across the room and landing near Shane's feet. Shane still has hold of Jason, whose face is a bloody pulp, by the throat, but he looks down and kicks the elf in the head like he's kicking a soccer ball.

I want to help. I want them to know I didn't mean for this to happen, but then Mikey closes the door and they're gone.

"Keep the hallway clear. Escort any guests to and from the rooms for the rest of the night," Liam says to the two bouncers who are standing in the hallway.

"Yes, Boss," they reply.

"Nobody is to know anything has happened. Make sure the customers have a good night, right?" Mikey adds.

"Always," one of them replies.

"Are you okay, Mrs. Ryan?" the other one asks me, his face full of concern.

"Yes, thank you," I say, forcing a smile.

"Shane and Conor will debrief you when they're done," Liam adds. Then he tucks my face back into the crook of his neck and walks down the hallway to the fire exit.

"The car is here, baby," he whispers. "We'll be home soon."

Mikey holds my hand while I sit on Liam's lap on the car ride home. Liam has his arms wrapped so tightly around me that I can barely move. We have hardly spoken since we left the club.

"I'm sorry I ruined our night," I whisper.

"No, baby. You didn't," Liam says softly, brushing my hair from my face. "You didn't ruin anything. I should never have let you out of my sight for even a second."

"I should have waited for you," I sniff. "Was that woman okay?"

"What woman?" he frowns at me.

"The woman who was crying earlier."

"I have no fucking idea, Jessie," he says with a frown. "The minute I realized you were missing my whole fucking world stopped turning."

Mikey puts his hand on the back of Liam's neck. "It wasn't your fault either, bro," he says.

"What are Shane and Conor going to do to them?"

"You already know, Red," Mikey replies.

I wipe away a tear that falls down my cheek. "It's my fault they have to do that."

"No. It's not," Liam says, hugging me tighter. "Those men hurt you, Jessie. They would have done way worse if we hadn't found you."

"Thank fuck we got to you so quick," Mikey says with a deep sigh.

"I'm so glad you did," I say with a shudder thinking of the threats Jason and his buddies made to me.

"Well, I knew you had to be in one of those rooms. We just had to get the keys and work our way through them," Liam tells me.

"Yeah, we saw some interesting sights opening the other doors before we found you, Red," Mikey says with a soft chuckle.

I smile at him but my heart is heavy with worry. Laying my head against Liam's chest, I hope that Shane and Conor are home soon.

As soon as we got home, Liam and Mikey briefed Chester on the evenings events while I took a quick shower — trying to wash away the reminder of Jason and his brother's grubby hands on my skin. I'm so relieved that it was only my neck they touched.

I rub the skin there subconsciously. My throat is a little sore but otherwise I'm fine. I just wish that Conor and Shane would come home so that I know they're fine too.

I climb into bed, pulling the covers over myself and a few moments later, Liam and Mikey walk into the room. Both of them are dressed in only their boxer shorts and Mikey carries a tray of hot chocolate.

"I put a little something special in for you, Red," he says with a wink. "It will help your sore throat."

"Irish whiskey, perhaps?" I ask and he smiles at me.

"Of course," Liam says as he climbs into bed beside me while Mikey sets the tray down on the nightstand before he slips beneath the covers too.

"You okay, baby?" Liam asks as he wraps a huge arm around me.

"Yeah," I lie. "I'm sorry I ruined Christmas."

"You did not," Mikey admonishes me. "Of all my Christmases, this doesn't rank in even the top twenty-five worst ones."

"Yeah. This Christmas is still epic and it's only just Christmas Eve," Liam adds with a chuckle.

I snuggle between them both. "I'm sorry you never had good Christmases growing up," I whisper.

I have only happy memories of my family before I was kidnapped by a psychopath when I was sixteen. Sometimes I forget how difficult my husband's childhoods were, particularly Liam and Mikey. Their mom was murdered by the man they believed was their father when they were just babies. Then he neglected, abused and mentally tortured them until Shane took them away from him when they were sixteen. Leaving Ireland and moving to New York.

"We did have that one Christmas, remember," Mikey laughs. "When Shane bought the house in Carrickfergus?"

"Yeah," Liam says with a smile. "How old were we?"

"Eleven," Mikey replies. "He was nineteen and Conor was fifteen."

"Oh, yeah. Conor was annoyed because he wanted to spend Christmas with his new girlfriend but Shane made him come with us. Poor kid had just discovered the joys of fucking," Liam laughs.

"So it was just the four of you for Christmas?" I ask.

"Yeah. We left on Christmas Eve. Shane had a tree and presents and everything. We had a great two days," Mikey replies.

"Yup. Until boxing day," Liam says with a shudder.

"Patrick found you all?" I ask them. He is Shane and Conor's biological father but not the twins, which they only found out about two years ago when Patrick died.

"Yeah. Shane had gone out for something and Patrick must have waited for him to leave because he showed up as soon as he left. He beat the shit out of the three of us and took me and Liam home," Mikey says matter of factly.

"It was the last time he ever laid a hand on Conor," Liam adds. "Because he stood up to him that day."

"Evil fuck stopped Shane coming into the house for about two months after, didn't he?" Mikey asks his brother.

Liam nods. "Uh-huh."

My heart aches for them and what they endured as children. Shane all but raised them. He was their protector. He and Conor were the only people to ever give them any love and affection and I can't imagine how hard it must have been for them all when their oldest brother wasn't allowed to see them.

"I'm sorry," I whisper.

"Don't be, baby. It was a long time ago," Liam says as he kisses my forehead. "And now we have you and our beautiful babies. You made Christmas magic for us again."

"You have for me too," I breathe.

There was a time when my only focus in life was finding the man who murdered my family and kept me prisoner for two years. All I wanted was to make him pay — and after that I had no future plans of happiness or family. Then I met my incredible Ryan brothers and my life changed forever.

"I love you."

"We love you too, Red," Mikey says softly.

I swallow the ball of emotion in my throat as I lie between the two of them, feeling safer and more loved than I have since I was a child. I only hope that their older brothers are safe right now, and that they can forgive me for what they're currently doing.

CHAPTER
EIGHT
JESSIE

Christmas Eve

I lay awake for hours but must have drifted off to sleep because I don't hear Shane and Conor come into the room.

"Everything okay, bro?" Liam asks and the sound of his voice rouses me.

"All sorted," Conor replies as he and Shane start undressing. They're wearing jeans and t-shirts rather than their tuxedos and I can't help but think of the reason why.

"I think I heard one of the twins waking up," Shane says. "Can you?"

"Sure," Liam says, nudging Mikey awake before rolling out of bed.

I check the clock and notice it's almost seven a.m.

Pulling back the covers, I go to climb out of bed too.

"Not you, sweetheart," Shane orders. "Stay right where you are."

"But I should help," I insist as uncertainty settles into the pit of my stomach. Shane looks super pissed while Conor is so quiet and can barely look at me.

"Yeah. You didn't get much sleep, Red," Mikey says with a yawn. "I felt you tossing and turning all night."

"Okay," I whisper as I lie back against the pillow and watch Shane and Conor pulling off the last of their clothes.

My heart races. Are they going to punish me? Together? I mean usually that's hot, bur right now I feel too fragile. Besides, it's not like I asked to be manhandled into a room with those creeps.

Mikey and Liam walk out of the room, closing the door behind them and my pulse quickens further. When they are naked, Shane and Conor climb into bed, one either side of me.

"I'm sorry," I almost cry.

"Don't, Jessie," Shane snaps, taking hold of my chin in his strong hand, he turns my face so he can look into my eyes. "I'm sorry, sweetheart. We all fucked up. Not you."

"W-what?" I stammer, aware of Conor's hand sliding onto my stomach.

"We never take our eyes off you, angel," he says before he kisses my shoulder softly. "That's the rule."

"But you can't always-"

"You should never have been in a position where any of those fucks could lay a finger on you, sweetheart. I'm sorry that they did."

"That's not your fault," I whisper as emotion balls in my chest. I thought they were mad at me, but they were mad at themselves.

"It will never happen again," Conor murmurs against my skin.

"Did you..." I don't finish the question.

"They're taken care of," Shane says before he slides his hand to my waist. "Turn on your side."

I shift onto my side until I'm facing him. Conor splays his hand on my stomach, pulling me against him so his chest is at my back as Shane presses a soft kiss on my lips.

"Can you forgive us, angel?" Conor asks as he nuzzles my neck.

"There's nothing to forgive."

"Thank you, sweetheart," Shane mumbles as his eyes close. "I'm so fucking tired."

"Me too," Conor yawns.

"What time do we have to be up for the Christmas Eve activities?" Shane asks and I smile.

Before I came into their lives they never really celebrated Christmas and I love how they are embracing my holiday spirit.

"Midday would be good," I suggest.

"That gives us five solid hours," Shane groans.

"Sounds like fucking heaven," Conor agrees.

"I should go help the twins with the twins."

"No," they say in unison.

"You're staying right here. Because I never sleep as well as when I have your gorgeous fucking body against mine," Shane adds.

"He speaks the truth," Conor agrees sleepily.

"Okay," I whisper, relieved to have them both home safe and not mad at me.

Smiling, I close my eyes and snuggle between the warmth of their hard bodies.

CHAPTER

NINE

MIKEY

"Dada. Dada," Ella chants as she waves her chocolate frosting covered fingers in the air.

"Mo. Mo," Finn squeals for more before he stuffs another fistful of frosting into his mouth.

"These babies will never sleep tonight," Jessie laughs as she wipes a blob of goo from Ella's hair. "They've eaten more sugar this afternoon than they have in their entire lives."

"Well, it was your idea to make Christmas cookies, Red," I remind her with a wink.

"It's a Christmas Eve tradition," she says as her cheeks turn pink.

Fuck, I love how she blushes at the slightest thing. As though she's not a deviant sex maniac under that sweet exterior.

"And is us wearing more cookies than we make part of our tradition, angel?" Conor asks as he looks down at his t-shirt and jeans which are covered in frosting, flour and cookie dough.

"Well, you do look kind of cute," she says with a shrug.

"And these babies look goddamn adorable," Liam adds as

he picks Ella up from her chair and she shrieks with laughter as she wipes more chocolate into his beard.

"They sure had fun," Shane laughs softly as he peels a squashed M&M from his jeans.

"They did," Jessie beams with pride.

She had a list of things she wanted us all to do on the twin's first Christmas Eve, including watching Elf, which the babies were less than impressed with. But they had fun rolling around the floor with Shane and me instead while Jessie watched the film with Liam and Conor. Then we went to the roof and made a snowman. After that we had hot chocolate and made Christmas cards, which Ella and Finn enjoyed because they got their hands and feet covered in paint. If that wasn't exhausting enough, then we made Christmas cookies. The result of which is now stuck to all of us and also scattered around the entire kitchen.

"I think they need a bath now though," Conor chuckles as he picks Finn up from his high chair, who protests at being parted from the chocolate frosting on his tray that he's yet to eat.

"Hey, buddy," Conor says calmly, rubbing his thumb over our son's cheek. "You can't eat any more sugar today, okay?"

Finn stops yelling, as though he understands what Conor is saying. He's not as vocal as Ella yet. She can say more than a dozen words, but all he can say is Ma, Da, no and mo — which means more, but damn that kid is as smart as a whip. He's gonna be just like his mom. He has her bright blue eyes and our dark hair, while Ella looks just like us Ryan boys, and she's as mischievous as us too. I can already tell that girl is going to give us a whole world of trouble, and I am so here for it.

I look at my brothers holding our kids - Jessie pulling more frosting out of Ella's hair while she tells her what a beautiful girl she is as Liam gently bounces her in his arms. Conor passes

Finn to Shane while he cleans some frosting from his beard and Finn giggles at the face Shane pulls at him. Of all of my brothers, I never thought I'd see Shane with kids of his own. I mean, he pretty much raised Liam, Conor and me, and I figured that would have been enough to put him off for life. But then we met Jessie and she turned our entire fucking worlds on their axis — in the best possible way. She has given me everything I didn't even know I wanted and then some.

"You okay?" she asks as she looks up at me and I realize I'm staring.

"Yep. Just wondering who's going to clean this kitchen up with me, is all."

"I'll help you, obviously," she says with a smile.

"Let's get these monsters cleaned up and in their Christmas pajamas," Liam says.

"You all have pajamas too," Jessie giggles, biting her lip in that adorable way that makes us unable to refuse her anything.

"Jessie!" Shane says with a roll of his eyes. "I'm not wearing pajamas, sweetheart."

"Me neither," Conor agrees.

"But they're Christmas pajamas. We all have to match. Please?" She clasps her hands together and flutters her eyelashes.

"We'll see," Shane grunts but we all know he's wearing the pajamas. And Conor will too. They would do anything to make her happy, just like Liam and I would.

My brothers took the twins for a bath about ten minutes ago and Jessie and I started tackling the mess that is the kitchen immediately after. We've made quick work of it together and all that's left to clean is the kitchen island.

She walks up beside me with a wet cloth in her hand and a bottle of organic cleaning spray that she makes herself because she doesn't want too many chemicals around our babies. She is way too fucking smart for me and I love every single fucking thing about her. And suddenly I realize I am alone with her. It's going to take my brothers at least another twenty minutes to bath our kids and then get themselves cleaned up.

And now I have zero interest in cleaning.

I pick up a giant blob of green frosting on my forefinger and smudge it onto her neck.

"Mikey!" she shrieks.

"Sorry, Red, my hand slipped," I say, grinning at her as she stands there pretending to be mad at me. "Here, let me get that for you," I offer, resting my hand on her hip and turning her to face me. I bend my head low, running my tongue over her collarbone and then up the soft skin of her throat until I collect all the frosting.

A tremor ripples through her body.

"Mmm. So fucking sweet," I murmur against her skin.

Her hands are in my hair now as she purrs like a kitten while I trail kisses over her neck. "Mikey," she whispers. "We're supposed to be cleaning."

"I am cleaning," I chuckle. "Cleaning you. You are very dirty, Red."

"So are you."

"About to get a whole lot fucking dirtier," I say, grabbing her by her ass cheeks and lifting her onto the counter, pushing myself between her thighs.

"Mikey. No," she laughs, trying to bat my hands away as I tickle her while I pull her dress up and off over her head.

I arch an eyebrow at her. "No?"

She stares at me, her eyes twinkling with mischief and delight as she chews on her bottom lip. I put a hand on her chest and push her to lie down flat on the counter top before dragging a stool over so I can sit down. Grabbing her ankles, I hook her legs over my shoulders.

She leans up on her elbows, staring at me with those beautiful blue eyes. "What are you doing?" she whispers.

"Oh you already know that, Red," I grin at her as I hook her panties to one side. I slide a finger through her silky wetness and she sucks in a stuttered breath that make her perfect tits jiggle for me. "You make me so fucking hard, you know that, right?"

"Y-yeah," she pants as I slip a finger inside her.

"And you're always so wet and ready for me." I thrust deeper. "Such a good fucking girl."

"Oh," she moans, lying flat on her back as I add another digit and rub her inner walls.

"You know what's sweeter than all this frosting?" I ask as I start to pepper kisses along the inside of her thighs.

"No."

"Your pussy, Red. You already knew that though." I nip her thigh lightly and she whimpers. "So fucking sweet," I growl as I breathe in the scent of her wet heat. I could fucking eat her all day every day. Every fucking meal and snack.

My cock throbs in my shorts, desperate to be inside her. But I gotta taste her first. Hooking a second finger into her panties, I pull them further aside, exposing her entire beautiful pussy to me. The soft, sucking sound of her wetness as I pump my fingers in and out of her makes my mouth water.

"God, Mikey," she breathes.

I bend my head closer and swirl my tongue over her clit while I keep finger fucking her. She gets wetter every time I thrust back inside her and I lap at her opening, drinking her in before I suck on her clit again.

Her sweet, salty arousal runs over my tongue and I swear it's the best damn thing I ever tasted. Thighs trembling, she moans softly and suddenly my balls are tightening and my spine is tingling and I feel like I'm gonna come just from eating her.

Reaching into my shorts, I grab hold of my cock and squeeze.

Sweet relief floods my body. *Fuck!*

Nothing beats being inside her hot, wet pussy, but right now she's on the edge of oblivion and I want to keep her here for as long as I can — with my name on her lips and in her head.

"Mikey," she groans my name again. "You feel so good."

"You taste so fucking good, Red," I growl as I start tugging on my rock hard dick, pumping the shaft to the same rhythm I'm drilling my fingers into her pussy.

"Fuck!" she hisses, threading her fingers through my hair. "So. Good."

I pull my fingers almost all the way out and seeing them thick with her cream makes my cock almost explode. Sliding them back in slowly, I tease her, sucking on the sensitive bud of flesh and keeping her teetering on the edge.

"Please?" she gasps, tugging on my hair as she rides my face and I take pity on her. Curling my fingers inside her as I suck harder, rimming her pretty little clit with my tongue and squeezing my dick harder until she is bucking and shaking and falling apart around me.

Her soft, breathy moans make me come apart, and as she's still grinding her sweet pussy on my mouth, I climax too, spilling cum all over my hand.

"Fuck!" I growl, my teeth nipping at her sensitive flesh.

She looks up at me, her skin pink and her eyes dark. "Did you just jack off while you were eating me?" she whispers wickedly.

I hold up my hand and show her the thick white ribbons

streaked over my knuckles. "I thought you were supposed to be helping me clean. You went and got me real messy."

She pushes herself up, a devilish grin on her face. "I can help you with that."

Then she takes my hand in hers and starts to lick my knuckles clean. Murmuring softly as she's cleaning me up, savoring the taste of me the way I just did her.

"Fuck, Red, that looks so fucking hot," I whisper.

Finally she sucks my thumb into her mouth, her tongue swirling around the tip as she stares into my eyes and now I'm sorry I didn't make her suck my cock. Her long dark lashes flutter and she looks so sweet and innocent — well she would be if she wasn't sucking my cum off my thumb.

"Keep sucking like that, Red, and I'll give you something else to put in that beautiful mouth of yours instead."

She releases my thumb from her mouth with a wet pop. "Fine by me," she purrs.

"You are a horny fucking minx, Mrs. Ryan," I say, wrapping my arms around her waist and lifting her from the counter. "And we need to finish cleaning this kitchen."

"I was trying to when you accosted me," she says, her eyes narrowed as she pretends to glare at me.

"I didn't hear no complaints," I say with a grin before I start to kiss her neck again. She still smells of chocolate frosting and cookies. I brush my fingers along her jawline and over her throat — the ones I just had inside her, so now she smells of her cum too.

"We should finish up and get ourselves cleaned up," she breathes even as she rakes her nails down my back, making me shiver.

"Goddammit, Jessie. I'm gonna bend you over this counter and fuck you instead."

"I knew you two would be fucking," Shane says with a sigh as he walks back into the kitchen.

I keep my arms wrapped around her and glare at him. "Clearly, we're not fucking."

He narrows his eyes at me in suspicion. "You just did though."

"No, we didn't," I insist.

He walks toward us, ignoring the fact that she's in my arms, he takes hold of her jaw, turns her head and kisses her. "You did something," he says, licking his lips and staring into her eyes.

"How do you know that?" she whispers.

He traces his pointer finger over her cheek. "Because your neck is all pink the way it is when you've just come."

"Maybe I'm just a little hot from you two kissing me?" she says with a shrug.

He shakes his head and then runs his nose along her jawline. "I can smell your cum on you, sweetheart, which means Mikey must have at least had his fingers in you."

I can't help laughing as her cheeks flush bright pink now. "Busted," I say to her with a wink. "We didn't fuck though. I mean I was about five seconds away from bending our wife over the nearest thing I could find and doing that, but we didn't."

Shane takes a deep breath as though the thought of doing that is distracting him from what he actually came in for.

"Did you need something?" Jessie asks him, trying to change the subject before one of us bends her over something.

He blinks at her. "I think Finn and Ella are about to crash after all that sugar. Their baths have wiped them out. I was gonna get them some milk and put them down a little early tonight."

"Yes, and then the adults Christmas Eve activities begin," I say with a grin.

"And they are presents, eggnog, hot chocolate and *A Christmas Carol*," Jessie says, shooting me a warning look.

"I know, Red."

"I'll come help with the twins," she says to Shane.

He arches an eyebrow at her. "We got it. Besides, I think you two need a shower."

A wicked grin spreads across my face.

"Separately," Shane adds.

"You are such a fucking buzzkill sometimes," I say to him.

He knows I'm joking but it doesn't stop him from slapping me across the back of my head.

"We'll finish up here, say goodnight to the twins and shower. Then we can all meet in the den in half an hour?" Jessie says excitedly.

God, I love how much this woman loves Christmas. She's like a shiny, sexy little elf.

"You think you can manage that?" Shane says to me.

I roll my eyes. "Like you wouldn't be buried in Jessie right now if it had been you two left on your own here?"

He sucks on his top lip as though he's deep in thought. "No. I would have taken her to my office instead where no-one would walk in on us," he finally says with a shrug.

"I'm standing right here, you know," Jessie protests.

"Don't pretend that you don't fucking love it, sweetheart," he says to her and her face breaks into another smile.

WHEN I'M SHOWERED, I pick up the Christmas pajamas Jessie has chosen for us. I suppose they're not that bad. The bottoms are red and white stripes and the top is like a Santa suit. I'm sure our kids will love them when we all wear them tomorrow, but for tonight I toss the t-shirt onto the bed and just pull on the pants. When I walk into the bedroom we all share, I see my brothers have had the same idea and are only wearing the bottoms too.

"Where is Jessie?" I ask.

"Just checking on the babies," Liam replies.

A few seconds later she walks into the room behind me and I spin around to see her dressed in a head to toe Mrs. Claus onesie with a hood.

"Where are your pajamas?" she asks us.

"Um. Wearing em," I say, pointing down at the ridiculous pants.

"You're supposed to wear the whole ensemble," she says with a roll of her eyes. "Now you don't look like Santa, just..." she chews on her lip as her eyes roam over the four of us.

"Just what, angel?" Conor asks.

"Just four super hot..." She waves her hand dismissively. "Don't worry. I can work with it," she adds with a soft sigh.

"But what the hell are you wearing, baby?" my twin asks as she walks toward the four of us.

"I'm Mrs. Claus," she whispers.

I pull her into my arms, spinning her around so I can check out her outfit. I look for snaps. Buttons? A zipper? A gap somewhere that I can get my hand in, but there isn't a single fucking one. "What fucking devious trickery is this, Red?" I growl.

"It's my onesie," she giggles.

"But how do I get into it?" I ask her as my brothers laugh — like this is funny.

She pulls a tiny flap near the base of her throat. "It's a concealed zipper, see?"

"I don't like it," I say with a shake of my head. "It's impenetrable."

"It's just for Christmas," she laughs.

"I still don't like it," I say as I wrap my arms around her and kiss her neck. "I like my hands on your skin."

She shivers in my arms and my cock twitches. "I like your hands on my skin too," she purrs.

Fuck! I didn't get enough of her in the kitchen. Not nearly enough. I want to fuck her so bad, but we have to go through her activity list first. I would much rather peel this goddam onesie off her, lay her down on that bed and do filthy things to her sexy little body all night long. I can guarantee my brothers will be thinking the same too. But she's so fucking excited about Christmas Eve and all of the things she has planned for us.

I can wait.

For her, I can.

For her I would wait a goddamn lifetime.

CHAPTER

TEN

JESSIE

After the twins have fallen asleep we head to the den to exchange presents. None of us are in need of much, and the boys never even used to exchange gifts at all, so we have agreed on one present each. They still didn't buy each other gifts though, which means I'll end up with four, and they only get one. They don't know about the extra ones I sneaked under the tree from the twins though.

I smile to myself when I think about tomorrow morning – Christmas with them and our babies is going to be something else. Last Christmas was magical. I was eight months pregnant and they spoiled me in so many ways. But I know that this one is going to be even better.

I sit cross legged on the floor and wait for them to open their gifts. "One at a time," I insist because I want to watch them all as they see what I got them.

They have more money than they could spend in three lifetimes and don't need anything at all — so I tried to choose gifts that would make them smile instead.

"Me first," Mikey insists, already tearing into the paper before the others have agreed, not that they would deny him.

He's an excitable little toddler at heart and it is one of the many reasons I love him. He pulls the soft fabric out of its wrapping and unfurls it, holding it up so he can see it in its full splendor. I can't see his face because it's hidden but then I hear him laughing loudly. He places the gift beside him and crawls across the floor to me.

"I fucking love it, Red," he grins before he kisses me on the lips.

"What does it say?" Conor asks as Liam picks it up.

"Don't kiss the chef," Liam chuckles as he turns the apron around to show everybody. "Unless your name is Jessie Ryan."

"Well your old one was getting a little worn. And that one seemed much more fitting," I say with a smile. Mikey always wears his 'Kiss the Chef' apron when he's cooking.

"It's perfect," he says with a wink.

"Me next?" Liam asks as he holds his own wrapped gift in his hands, and Shane and Conor nod their agreement.

He opens the paper carefully and pulls out the framed map and certificate before he reads it. "You named a star after me?" he asks with a smile so big that it makes me feel warm and fuzzy all over. He is such a sensitive soul.

"Yes. And the map is of where it was in the sky the night you first kissed me and changed our lives forever." I blush at the memory making his brothers laugh.

He shakes his head and stares down at the frame in his hands.

Shane catches my eye and winks at me. *Written in the stars.*

"I love it, baby," Liam says when he looks up again. "It's the best gift I've ever gotten."

"Might I remind you of the fucking red Porsche I bought you when you were twenty-one?" Mikey asks incredulously.

"Nothing compared to this, bro. Sorry," Liam laughs as he places the frame on the floor beside him.

95

"You're up next, Con," Shane says.

Conor smiles at me as he unwraps the paper. When he pulls out the book, he runs his hand over the soft leather. I see his Adam's apple bob in his throat as he swallows.

"It's the Maude translation. First edition," I tell him. "I know you wanted to read it to the babies now that you've finished *The Grapes of Wrath*."

Some people might question his choice of reading material, but I swear he could read those babies a takeout menu and they'd still be mesmerized by his deep, soothing voice. I love when he reads to me too and he used to read me this book, *Anna Karenina*, when we first met.

"It's fucking perfect, angel. Thank you," he says as he looks up at me, his eyes shining with happiness.

"Shane's turn," Mikey says excitedly and my heart flutters in my chest. This is either going to be as funny as hell or a complete disaster. Suddenly, I'm worried it's going to be the latter.

I press my lips together so that I don't giggle as I watch Shane unwrapping his gift. He tears at the red glittery paper and tosses it onto the floor before opening the small black cardboard box.

When he pulls out the contents I have to pinch the inside of my thigh to stop myself from laughing out loud. His brows knit into a frown as he rolls the thick rubber ring between his thumb and forefinger.

"It's a cock ring," I whisper, biting down on my bottom lip to stop the giggle escaping.

He looks up at me and arches one eyebrow. "I know what it is, sweetheart, but what I don't understand is why you bought it for me."

"They make erections harder and last longer," Mikey says nonchalantly and the look Shane gives him almost makes me pee my onesie. My cheeks hurt with the effort of not laughing.

"So why didn't everyone get one?" he asks me.

"Well, you did turn forty this year," I whisper and his entire face darkens.

"What the fuck?" he growls and I'm starting to wish I'd just given him his actual present instead of this one which Mikey convinced me would be too funny to pass up. His brothers stare at him and I can't stop myself. I am going to burst if I hold this in any longer. The look on his face is priceless.

I hold onto my sides as a snigger escapes my lips. Before I can tell him that I have his real present under the tree, he pounces on me from halfway across the room, pinning me flat to the floor with his hands clamped around my wrists.

He rocks his hips against me, his hard length digging into my abdomen as I giggle uncontrollably. "Does this feel like I need help getting hard, Jessie?"

Conor, Liam and Mikey start laughing too and I snort hysterically, squirming in Shane's grip as he rubs his jaw over my neck, tickling my soft skin.

"Does it?" he asks as he presses me flatter to the floor before one of his hands slides over my ribs and he starts to tickle me.

"Shane!" I shriek with laughter. "Stop! It was Mikey. He made me do it."

"Wow. Way to throw me under the bus, Red. Remind me never to take you to a negotiation," Mikey says with an exaggerated sigh.

"I'm not surprised this was your idea," Shane says as he looks at his younger brother. He's still holding onto the offending rubber band and he tosses it at Mikey. It bounces off his head and rolls under the sofa.

"What? I'd wear it," Mikey says with a shrug.

"It would be way too big for you, son," Shane laughs darkly

before he turns his attention back to me as I lie beneath him on the floor barely able to control myself. He shifts between my thighs until his cock is nudging at my pussy. "Did you think that was funny, sweetheart?" he whispers, his hot breath dusting over my cheek.

"Kinda," I grin at him.

"You looking for a spanking? Is that it?"

"You can't spank me on Christmas Eve," I protest.

"No?" He narrows his eyes at me.

"No. It's not on the permitted list of activities," I snigger.

"You're right it's not," he runs his nose along my jawline "So how about I fuck you instead? Right here, right now, sweetheart? Because if you think I need a cock ring clearly I need to remind you that I can fuck you longer and harder than any man in this room."

Sweet baby Jesus! Yes please! "We can't," I say instead even as I grind myself against him. "You haven't had your real present yet."

"And Jessie hasn't had hers," Liam adds.

"Jessie is about to get hers," Shane says as his eyes burn into mine.

I swallow hard. I can't figure out if he's amused, mad, horny — or all three. "Your real present is under the tree," I whisper. "The cock ring was just a joke. I promise."

He narrows his eyes at me, but there is a wicked glint in them that makes my insides melt like warm butter. He's not mad at all.

"Here it is," Liam says as he rummages under the tree and pulls out another gift wrapped in the red glittery paper.

Shane releases my wrists and pushes himself up, taking the gift from Liam, he starts to unwrap it, but he remains straddling me the entire time. His knees pinned against my hips so I can't move. When he unwraps this one he grins at me.

"It's Italian. They only make a dozen of them a year. Feel how soft it is?" I say.

"Hmm," he murmurs his agreement as he runs his hand over the soft, black leather. "You'll be feeling how soft it is."

Heat pools in my core at the meaning behind that statement. "Now you will always think of me when you take off your pants."

"Already do," he says with a smile before leaning down and kissing me. "Thank you, sweetheart."

My breath catches in my throat. As much as I enjoy pushing his buttons, I love to see that smile even more. "You're welcome."

"Time for Jessie's presents," Mikey says excitedly, interrupting the moment.

"I don't know," Shane says as he sits up and then pulls me onto his lap. My very own sexy Santa. "I don't think our Jessie has been a good enough girl for presents."

I roll my eyes. Did I say Santa? More like sexy Satan.

"I have been good," I insist and Conor and Liam laugh softly in the background while Mikey starts to rummage beneath our huge Christmas tree.

Shane tucks my hair behind my ear. "Well, not even counting that bratty little eye roll, shall we add up all of your little misdemeanors from the past few days?"

"What misdemeanors?" I say with a flutter of my eyelashes.

He arches one eyebrow at me. "The tattoo?"

"How is that a misdemeanor?"

"You kept it from us, angel," Conor says.

"Because it was a surprise," I insist.

"Yeah? But rigging the security feed so that we wouldn't see what you were doing wasn't, was it, sweetheart?"

My cheeks flush pink.

"You think we didn't know about that?" Conor chuckles.

"Oh, you're in trouble, baby," Liam adds with a soft laugh.

"Naughty, Red," Mikey says. "More of a felony than a misdemeanor, I'd say, bro."

"Hmm," Shane agrees as he rubs a hand over his jaw.

"How did you know about that?" I ask.

"Because you know we always watch you. How else would you have gone through with your little surprise if you didn't do something to the feed downstairs?"

I open my mouth to respond but nothing comes out. I have no comeback and should have known he would realize what I'd done.

"That was incredibly dangerous, sweetheart. What if something had happened to you?" Shane goes on.

"I was in our basement. Chester was going to be there," I protest as my blush deepens.

"I don't care. One of us has eyes on you at all times. That's the rule."

"Yeah, baby," Liam agrees with him.

I look at the concerned faces of Conor and Liam and then back at Shane. "So why are you only bringing this up now? Why didn't you say something the other day?"

Shane trails his fingertips over my cheek. "Because Conor was with you. You would never have gotten to that basement alone. Besides, then you went and floored me with that beautiful tattoo and..." he trails off and looks at Conor.

"That leads us to your other little indiscretion," Conor says, narrowing his eyes at me. "Making me come in front of Gia when I warned you not to."

I stifle a giggle. "I don't think I can be held accountable for your inability to control yourself," I say, trying to keep a straight face.

Shane laughs, the sound rumbling through him and making me shake on his lap.

Conor narrows his eyes at me. "Really, angel?" he challenges me.

"Really."

"Not to mention wearing the tiniest, tightest mini skirt possible when you went to work at the club the other night, and giving me a three hour boner," Shane goes on.

"It's the only black mini I own," I say with a shrug. "Conor chose it for me."

"I did," Conor admits with a wicked grin.

"You realize how many guys saw her in that sexy little skirt the other night, Con?" Shane asks and suddenly Conor's face darkens.

"Fuck," he growls.

"Am I wasting my time pulling all these gifts out?" Mikey asks as he sits back on his heels. "Because our girl has been so bad."

"I have not," I insist.

"Then there was the incident at Callie's," Liam adds.

I scowl at him. "I am definitely not responsible for that."

"I kinda think you are, baby," he says, winking at me and making heat coil up my spine.

"And now we have a hideous purple chair in our guest bedroom," Shane laughs.

"I quite like it," I say with a shrug.

"And the dress," Shane goes on.

"Oh, the dress," Mikey groans as he pokes his head back under the tree and both Liam and Conor voice their agreement.

"The dress?" I blink in confusion.

"Yes, the dress, sweetheart. The one that you wore last night. The one that hugged every inch of you?"

"It was just a dress," I whisper.

"That was not *just* a dress, angel. It was fucking..." Conor shakes his head.

"It was way too distracting," Shane growls as he presses his lips close to my ear.

I swallow hard.

"Then there's the pajamas," Liam adds as he pulls at the waistband of his red and white striped pants.

"And let's not forget that fucking monstrosity," Mikey says as he crawls out from under the tree and looks at me.

"What monstrosity?" I ask with a frown.

Shane grabs a wad of my pajama fabric in his fist. "I think he means this, sweetheart."

"Oh," I giggle.

"So, what are we gonna do with all these then?" Mikey asks as he looks down at the pile of wrapped gifts beside him.

"Are they all for me? There are way too many. We agreed one each," I say.

"Like you stuck to that rule, Red," Mikey laughs. "I see our other gifts under there too."

"They're just little ones from the babies."

"These are just little," Mikey replies as he picks up a small gold parcel before he looks at his brothers and grins wickedly. "Are we gonna let her open them?"

I look at Shane. "What do you say, Santa?"

He cups my face in his hands, his eyes dark as they burn into mine. "Are you our good girl?" he asks in that low timbre that has a direct path to my ovaries.

Holy fuck!

"Yes," I purr.

"Then I suppose we are," he slaps my ass and shifts me off his lap.

Then I sit cross legged on the floor and my husbands watch as I start to unwrap the first of my gifts.

I'M SITTING on the floor, my back against the sofa, surrounded by swathes of glittery paper and gift tags and with a pile of gifts on my lap. Eight new sets of underwear — two from each of them. A pair of leopard print Louboutins with a six inch heel. Eight, yes eight, tubes of lube in a variety of different flavors. A flogger. A paddle. A vibrating egg that is controlled by a remote app they have already installed on their phones. Massage oil. And a silk blindfold. There is definitely a theme here. Though I don't know why I expected any less.

"Thank you so much," I say, my cheeks hurting from smiling. "I love them all."

"Good," Liam leans across and kisses my cheek.

"These are just your naughty presents, Red," Mikey says with a grin. "You can open your real ones tomorrow."

I stare at him. *My real ones?* "What? No. We agreed one gift each and you already bought too many. We said tomorrow would be about the babies." I protest.

"I believe you agreed to that all on your own, angel," Conor says.

"No. We all said one gift each."

"We agreed you would get us one gift," Shane reminds me.

"But that's not fair. I didn't get you guys hardly anything."

"We don't need anything, Red," Mikey says with a shrug.

"Neither do I," I protest.

I'm about to go on protesting when Liam jumps up and pulls me into his arms. "You have given us everything we have ever wanted, baby. Please let us spoil you a little. It makes us happy."

I stare into his beautiful dark eyes. How the hell do I stay mad at him, or any of them?

"You won't fool me next year," I say with a fake scowl.

"We already know what we want next year," Mikey mumbles, earning him a withering look from Shane.

"Eggnog?" Conor shouts as he pushes himself to his feet and the conversation changes before I have a chance to ask Mikey what he means.

"And cookies," I say with a smile.

"Eggnog and cookies," Mikey rolls his eyes.

"What? I'm sure they'll be perfect together," I say with a shrug.

"I want some of the cookies Mikey made," Shane says, winking at me.

I put my hands on my hips and glare at him. "Are you saying you don't want the cookies me and our children made?"

"I'm saying exactly that, sweetheart," he laughs.

Liam wraps his arm around my waist and kisses my neck. "I'll have your cookies, baby," he whispers.

"Later, sex pest," Conor says giving him a nudge on the arm. "Let's get this cleared up."

"I'll go help Mikey." I smile and then he and I head to the kitchen while Conor, Liam and Shane tidy up the wrapping paper.

CONOR TAKES the glass of eggnog from my hand and then pulls me to sit on his lap, wrapping his huge arms around me and nuzzling my neck, I practically purr in contentment as I snuggle against his hard chest.

"Hey, I forgot to tell you all, I had a call from some magazine wanting to interview me," he says nonchalantly before taking a sip of his drink.

I open my mouth, about to ask him half a dozen questions, but his brothers get there before me.

"What magazine?" Mikey asks.

"What did you say?" Shane says as at the same time.

"I said, fuck no," Conor replies with a frown. "Why the hell would some magazine want to put me in it?"

"Um, because you're a super successful, handsome owner of the hottest nightclub in New York," I say.

"Part owner," Mikey adds.

"Yeah, well when I said no, she asked if any of you were available. I said fuck no on your behalf too."

"You sure it was a magazine and not someone fishing for information?" Shane asks with a scowl — always so suspicious, although I suppose he has reason to be.

Conor shrugs. "Seemed legit. Said she was from that magazine Jessie reads. Ten things I want to know about you, or some shit."

"The *Ten things you didn't know* column," I squeal. "I love that feature. It's one of my favorites. I can totally see why they would want to interview one of you guys for it."

Liam reaches forward and shuffles through the magazines beneath the coffee table before he finds the Christmas edition of Fever magazine. I have it on a monthly subscription and love to read it at night lying on the sofa with my head on Mikey's lap.

"I would so do that interview," Mikey says with a chuckle.

"You will not," Shane says with a scowl.

"It's not like they ask anything deep and meaningful. It's all pretty lighthearted stuff," I tell him.

"I don't want anyone knowing anything about any of us," Shane says and Conor nods his agreement while Liam flicks through the magazine before he finds the regular feature.

"So, Michael Ryan," Liam says in a thick New York accent. "Successful businessman. Father of two. Sex god?"

Mikey sits forward in his seat, puffing out his chest as he prepares for his big interview. "Yup."

"What do you wear in bed?" Liam asks in his regular voice.

"My wife," Mikey replies without a seconds thought, making his brothers laugh.

"Favorite thing to eat?" Liam asks.

"My wife's pussy."

"Mikey," I say as my cheeks turn pink.

"It's true, Red," he frowns at me then he turns back to his twin. "Next question."

"Favorite drink?"

"The sweet stuff that comes out of my wife's pussy," Mikey answers and my cheeks redden further.

"That's not a drink," I say.

"I drink it," Mikey insists. "I'd bottle it and take it in a flask to work with me if I could."

"You have to choose an actual drink. My pussy can't be your answer to everything."

"But your pussy is the answer to everything, sweetheart," Shane says with a wicked grin.

His words make warmth roll through my core, but I keep trying to argue my point anyway. "It's not a drink," I whisper.

"Then let's put it to a vote," Mikey suggests. "A drink is a liquid, right? Best liquid you've ever tasted?" He looks between each of his brothers and then back at me.

I fake a scowl at him and he flashes his eyebrows at me.

Conor sips his eggnog. "This stuff is pretty good, actually," he says, running his tongue over his bottom lip as he stares into my eyes. "But nowhere near as sweet as you, angel."

"I agree, baby," Liam adds while Shane sips his eggnog and winks at me over the rim of his glass.

"Favorite thing to do at Christm-"

"My wife," Mikey says before Liam has even finished the question.

Shane grins wickedly while Liam tries to keep a straight face, meanwhile Conor is chuckling softly and the sound rumbles through his entire body. Mikey winks at me and I roll my eyes.

"You're my favorite thing to do on any holiday though, Red," he insists. "Any season. Any time really."

I can't help but smile at him. "Can you answer the next ones properly?"

"I am answering properly," he says with a frown before he looks to Liam again who is scanning the magazine page with a devious look on his face.

"Favorite travel destination?" Liam asks.

"My wife's pussy," Mikey replies without missing a beat and his three brothers burst into laughter.

"That is not a travel destination!" I exclaim, which only makes his brothers laugh harder.

Conor's entire body is shaking now as he keeps his arms wrapped around me. It's a good thing his eggnog glass is empty or it would be spilling all over the two of us.

"It is," Mikey insists. "If I wanted to be inside it right now, which I do, obviously, then I would have to stand and walk across the room to get there. That is the very definition of traveling, Red."

I shake my head as a soft laugh bubbles in my throat. Seeing my four husbands so relaxed and happy is the best Christmas present I could ever ask for. "You're a deviant, Mikey Ryan."

He stands and walks over to me, bending his head and brushing his lips over my cheek. "But I'm your deviant, Jessie Ryan," he growls in my ear. His hand slides over my neck until he finds the zipper of my onesie and flicks the tip of it between his thumb and forefinger.

"We haven't watched the movie yet," I whisper.

"I know," he says, his warm breath dusting over my cheek and making me shiver. "I was just on my way to fill everyone's eggnog."

He stands tall again and takes Conor's glass from him. "Then can I have a hot chocolate please?" I flutter my eyelashes at him.

"Sure."

"With marshmallows?"

"Anything for you, Red," he leans and gives me a soft kiss on the lips before leaving the room.

～

Mikey switches off the TV and suddenly I feel all of my husband's eyes on me.

"That was the final thing on your list of Christmas Eve activities, baby," Liam says with a smile.

"Hmm," Conor agrees as he fingers the zip of my onesie. "Now it's time for our list."

"Your list?" I whisper as he starts to pull down my zipper. "But Christmas Eve is almost over."

"Oh it's not a big list, angel," he chuckles as he slips a hand inside my pajamas, cupping one of my breasts and squeezing gently. "You'll have time to get to sleep before Santa comes."

Shane has crossed the room now and is kneeling in front of us. "But only if you're a good girl, sweetheart," he adds with a grin. "You gonna be a good girl for us?"

His words vibrate through my entire body as Conor pulls my zipper all the way down.

"Y-yes," I whimper as wet heat sears between my thighs and my entire body starts to tremble.

"She's always a good girl, aren't you, angel?" Conor whispers in my ear as he turns me on his lap so I'm facing frontward before he begins peeling my onesie off over my arms.

I blow out a long breath as Shane takes hold of the fabric and starts to pull it over my hips and thighs. His dark green eyes burn into mine as he works the soft material over my legs and a few seconds later I'm completely naked as I sit on Conor's lap.

"No panties, Red?" Mikey asks.

"Not with pajamas," I whisper as my eyes stay fixed on Shane's and I wonder what's going through his devious mind.

"I'm gonna need you to hold her for me, Con," Shane growls as his hands slide up my inner thighs. "I don't want her to be able to move."

Holy fuck!

Conor chuckles softly as he spreads my legs wider apart and hooks my feet beneath his calves. When my legs are secure, he takes hold of my wrists and places them behind my back, before wrapping his arms around me tightly so that I'm completely restrained. When Shane presses his palms against the top of my inner thighs, I can barely move at all.

My heart hammers against my ribcage as Shane dips his head close to my pussy. "You smell so fucking good, Hacker," he breathes. "Why are you soaking wet already?"

"Because Conor was kissing my neck and grabbing my ass through the whole movie."

"I was," Conor admits.

"Can't say I blame you, bro," Mikey says as he sits on the sofa beside Liam watching me and his brothers intently.

"Hmm," Shane mumbles before he starts to pepper soft kisses over the top of my thighs. I try to squirm in Conor's grasp but I'm held still by the two of them.

"Why don't you want me to move?" I whisper.

Shane looks up at me. "You know why, sweetheart." He presses a soft kiss directly on my clit and I shudder. "Because I want to wear Mikey's favorite drink."

I hear Mikey laughing but the sound seems far away as I focus on Shane's expert tongue as he swirls it over my sensitive flesh. "Shane," I groan his name softly.

"I know, sweetheart," he murmurs against my skin.

Conor nuzzles my neck while Shane sucks and nibbles on my pussy and my head starts to swim as pleasure builds in my core and starts to coil through my limbs.

"Tell her what we were going to do to her in the basement of the club, Con," Mikey says.

"Fuck yeah," he hisses. "We were gonna tie you up, angel. And then we were just gonna take turns fucking you and making come all night."

"Oh my God," I moan. That sounds so hot. "I wanna do that."

"We'll do it soon," he promises as he kisses my neck.

"I'm gonna..." I come unexpectedly, my body shaking and shuddering in Conor's arms. Shane growls his appreciation as he laps up my juices.

"Damn, angel, I need to fuck you right now," Conor grunts in my ear and I shiver. "I'm gonna have to let her move while I get inside her, bro," he says to Shane who mumbles his agreement while he goes on sucking my clit.

Conor snaps his fingers and Liam tosses him a bottle of lube from the coffee table. He coats his shaft quickly and expertly before lifting me slightly and spreading my legs wider using his feet. His cock presses against the seam of my ass and I whimper as he breaches my opening.

"I know," he whispers in my ear, "Focus on Shane while I slide inside you, okay?"

"Yes," I gasp as he sinks deeper while his older brother slips a finger inside my pussy. "Oh, God," I whine, trying to buck my hips but the two of them hold me firmly in place.

Shane swirls his tongue over my clit and sucks my sensitive flesh at the same time as he massages his finger against that spot inside me that makes me whimper shamelessly — all while Conor fucks my ass. It's too much sensation. I can't handle any more...

"Oh, holy fuck," I groan as my orgasm bursts out of me so violently that I hear it splashing onto the wooden floor.

"That's my good girl," Conor growls in my ear as he goes on fucking me through it and the deep groan that rumbles through his chest tells me he's found his own release too.

Shane pulls back, wiping his jaw with a sweep of his huge hand.

"Look at me, sweetheart," he says, the low timbre of his voice rumbling through my bones.

I stare at him, my eyes locked on his.

"Look at me on my fucking knees for you."

I suck in a stuttered breath.

"Do you see what you do to me? To all of us?" he goes on.

"You make us fucking feral, Red," Mikey adds with a low growl as he walks over to us. I look up at him now and his eyes darken. His muscles flex as he crosses his arms and I stare at his hard, tattooed body.

Liam crosses the room too until he's standing beside his twin. "We know you were hoping for a some sleep tonight," he says with a wicked grin.

"But that's not happening," Conor says.

"You're getting fucked by all of us," Liam adds.

I lick my lips as my heart starts to flutter in my chest and my internal organs turn to liquid chocolate. I'm surrounded by these four huge, powerful, violent men who are all staring at me like they want to eat me alive. Conor is still holding me so tightly that I can barely move.

I tremble in his arms. I guess I must look like a frightened rabbit in a lion's den.

Except I am not a rabbit. I am a lion too.

CHAPTER
ELEVEN

JESSIE

Liam holds out his hand to me. "You remember where this all began, baby?" he says, his eyes sparkling with mischief and happiness. "This den."

"That sofa," Mikey adds with a wicked grin as he nods toward the huge couch he and Liam were just sitting on.

Conor releases me from his embrace and I take Liam's hand and allow him to pull me up onto shaky legs until he has me wrapped in his arms.

He trails his lips over my ear. "You remember how nervous you were about taking us both together?"

"Yes," I blush at the memory.

"And now you take us all," he chuckles.

"And so fucking well, Red," Mikey says as he presses his body against my back.

"You gonna take us all in here tonight?" Liam whispers as his hand slips between my thighs and he rubs my swollen, throbbing clit with the slightest of pressure, but it's enough to make my legs buckle and Liam has to hold me up.

"Yes," I pant against his neck and he lifts me, wrapping my

legs around his waist and carrying me over to the rug in front of the fire.

He lays me down on it and then pushes himself up, standing over me as Mikey and Shane walk over and join us. Conor leaves the room and I figure he must be going to clean up so he can fuck me again too.

How is it that I can never get enough of these men? My limbs ache. My pussy throbs. My ass is tender, but I still want more. I want everything they can give me.

The three of them stare down at me, still dressed in their Christmas pajama pants.

Mikey rubs a hand over his jaw. "We were gonna tie her up last night, right?"

"Yep," Shane replies as his eyes roam over every inch of my body.

"I still wanna," Mikey says and when I look at him, he's pulling a huge swathe of thick green tinsel from the mantel-piece. He holds it up for his brothers to inspect and they both nod their approval.

"Our girl does look good in green," Shane laughs.

I arch an eyebrow at them. "You're going to tie me up with tinsel?"

"Looks like," Liam laughs too as Shane and Mikey drop to their knees beside my head.

"Hands," Shane orders and I hold them out in front of me, allowing Mikey to wrap the tinsel around my wrists.

I squirm and giggle as the strands dance over my breasts ever time he loops the length through my arms.

"Stop it, Red," Mikey grins at me.

"I can't help it. It tickles," I laugh harder.

"A little help, bro?" he says to Shane.

Shane rolls his eyes. "You're such a fucking amateur," he

says with a shake of his head as he places his huge hands on my waist and holds me still.

But as Mikey resumes tying me up, Shane wiggles his fingers against my sides and I squeal with laughter, curling my knees up to my chest as I try to stop him from tickling me.

"Shane!" Mikey sighs. "I'm trying to fucking tie her up here."

Tears roll down my cheeks as I writhe on the floor as Shane goes on pressing his fingers into my incredibly ticklish ribs.

"I'm not doing anything," Shane protests.

Mikey lets the tinsel go and sits back on his heels. "Is this about the cock ring?"

"Of course not," his older brother replies with a smug grin. This is so about the cock ring. "It's not my fault you don't know how to properly restrain our wife."

"You do it then, smart ass," Mikey challenges him.

"Fine," Shane says, winking at me as he lets go of my waist and takes hold of the end of the tinsel which is dangling from my wrists.

He has it tied securely almost before I can take another breath let alone have another fit of giggles.

Mikey looks on in admiration at his eldest brother's handiwork while I lie here waiting for whatever is coming next.

"And that's how it's done, son," Shane says to him with a wink.

"You are a cocky fucker, you know that?" Mikey says with a shake of his head.

"I sure am," he laughs as he grabs hold of the tinsel binding my wrists and lays down. "Come here, sweetheart and we'll remind my little brother just how much of a fucker I am."

He pulls me up and I straddle him, placing my bound hands on his chest as he pulls his striped pajama pants down enough to free his cock. I whimper with need as I press myself against it, coating him in the slick juices he just wrung from my body.

"You gonna ride me like my good girl?" he growls as he grabs my hips and shifts my position so that he's sliding into my pussy.

"Yeah," I groan, sinking all the way down and letting him fill me.

Mikey kneels behind me, between Shane's legs. "You look so good when you're being fucked, Red," he whispers in my ear. "I'm gonna fuck you with him, okay."

I nod my agreement, overwhelmed by the sensations of his hands on me and his mouth on my ear while Shane rocks his hips deeper inside me.

"You want the lube?" Conor says as he comes up beside us.

"Nope," Mikey laughs softly. "I'm not gonna need any where I'm going."

"Jesus!" Shane hisses as my pussy squeezes around his cock.

"Are you both...?" I whimper as heat floods my entire body. I'm going to pass out any moment now and miss the rest of Christmas because I'll be in an orgasm induced coma.

"Yeah. You can take us both, can't you?" Mikey growls as he slides a hand over my hips and onto my stomach, holding me still as he presses his cock against my pussy opening. I am so full of Shane I have no idea how he's going to fit too and my whole body tenses.

"Relax, sweetheart," Shane soothes, pulling me to lie flat against his chest and looping my bound wrists over his head and around his neck. "We would never hurt you."

"I know," I whisper as I press my cheek against his hard chest.

Mikey nudges the tip of his cock inside me and I suck in a deep breath at the burning stretch.

"That's my good girl," Shane whispers and my entire body

melts against him. Damn devil knows exactly what those words do to me.

"Oh fuck, Red. You feel so good like this," Mikey groans.

"Oh, God," I whimper as he pushes deeper until I'm so full I feel like I can hardly breathe.

Shane wraps both of his arms around me, holding me tight to him as he starts to rock his hips up slightly. The pressure of Mikey's cock tight against his as he moves makes me feel every single millimeter of him. And when Mikey starts moving too, their thick lengths massage my inner walls, rubbing against every nerve ending inside me and the feeling is so exquisite – so much, that I sob.

Both of them stop moving immediately.

Shane cups my chin in his hand and looks at me, worry darkening his handsome features. "Sweetheart?"

I suck in a shaky breath that vibrates through my body. "I'm good. It feels so good. But it's just so... much."

"You want us to stop?" Mikey leans over me, pressing a soft kiss on the back of my neck.

"No, I just need a second," I say.

Suddenly Conor and Liam are lying either side of their brothers. Conor leans in and brushes his lips over the tears on my cheek. "You're incredible, angel."

"Yeah, baby," Liam adds. "You're taking those cocks like a champ."

That makes me laugh and then Shane and Mikey start to laugh too, and the sound vibrates through their bodies and into mine until I'm sandwiched between them feeling completely boneless.

"I'm ready," I breathe.

"Good, 'cause I'm about to come from being squeezed so tight in your pussy, sweetheart," Shane says, giving me a kiss on the forehead before he presses my face against the crook of his neck and then starts to fuck me again.

The euphoria tears through my body, wave after wave of pleasure and pain and pleasure again as I have another squirting orgasm that soaks all of us.

I lie between them, unable to move or even speak as they fuck me through every delicious second.

"I'm gonna come," Shane grunts and Mikey pulls out as his older brother finishes deep inside me.

"Fuck, Red," Mikey growls as he finishes on my backside, leaving warm ribbons of his release on my ass cheeks. "You look so good covered in my cum." Then his hands are on me, massaging my lower back and rubbing his arousal into my skin like it's lotion.

I moan softly as his strong hands work gently into my muscles. Shane cups my chin and tilts my head so he can kiss me, lazily tongue fucking me as his hands glide over my back and shoulders. Between him and Mikey they make me feel completely boneless. Like a giant pile of Jell-o.

I don't know how long we stay like that with Shane kissing me while him and Mikey soothe my aching muscles. I'm in some kind of space that I can't explain. That blissed out place between sleeping and waking where you're aware of everything but remain in a cocoon of warmth and happiness.

"You okay, Red?" Mikey asks, pressing his lips to my ear.

Shane breaks our kiss and I drop my head back to his chest. "Yes," I purr.

"Good, because you know we're not done yet," Shane whispers as he slides his cock out of me and releases a rush of our cum that soaks him. "Fuck, sweetheart," he groans. "You're gonna need to hydrate before round two."

Mikey chuckles and I feel him pushing himself to a standing

position. "I'll go grab the Gatorade and meet you all in the bedroom."

"You can come with me, angel," Conor whispers as he pulls me from Shane's arms and scoops me into his.

I loop my still tinsel bound arms over his head and around his neck as I press my face against his skin. Damn! He smells so good I could lick him from head to toe. "Sounds good to me."

CHAPTER
TWELVE
LIAM

Trailing soft kisses over her stomach, I brush my fingers over Jessie's sensitive clit and it makes her back arch in pleasure as she moans loudly.

"Liam," she hisses as I press a little firmer.

"I know, baby," I murmur against her skin.

She is lying on Conor, her back against his chest as he fucks her. He starts to rub her clit now and she bucks in his arms. She's almost taken as much as she can handle from all four of us but she has a little more to give. We push her so hard but she handles it all so well.

I look up at my older brother. I want inside her. For as long as I've been fucking women, I've shared them with my twin, but never with my two older brothers before we met Jessie. Despite that we're all as in tune when it comes to her.

Conor slides his cock out of her pussy and she whimpers in frustration.

"Only for a second, angel," he chuckles as he pushes inside her ass instead, already lubricated from the four us fucking her tonight.

I slide two fingers into her hot pussy at the same time.

"Oh, fuck!" she hisses.

"Good girl, sweetheart. You take us all so fucking well," Shane says as he and Mikey watch us, their hands kneading her breasts.

I feel the effect of my older brother's words in her pussy as she squeezes me tight. Our girl has a massive praise kink and we all know it.

I'm the last to fuck her pussy tonight but that's fine with me. It means I get her to myself for a little while and I can savor every tremor and moan that my cock in her pussy will wring from her body.

"Fuck, angel," Conor groans as he thrusts deeper inside her and the sounds he makes tell me he's just blown his load.

"Conor," she whimpers his name now as he pulls his cock out of her ass.

As soon as Conor is done, Shane and I slide her off him and onto the bed and she groans in frustration as I pull my fingers out of her. Chasing her next orgasm despite how many times we've already made her come tonight. I love keeping her on the edge of them and then watching her bright blue eyes roll in her head as she comes apart for me.

"Soon, baby," I chuckle as I nestle between her thighs, my cock at her opening. Pushing the tip into her silky wet center is all I need to do to make her wrap her legs around my waist and her arms around my neck. It's just me and her now. My brothers watch but the next time she comes it will all be for me.

I sink all the way inside her, relief flooding through me at being encased in her tight pussy. "You're still so fucking snug, baby," I groan as I drive deeper. "Even after all my brothers fucked you."

"Oh! Liam. You feel," she gasps. "So. Good."

"I love fucking you, Jessie," I grunt as I bury my face in her neck and nail her to the mattress, finally tipping her over the edge.

My balls almost explode when she screams my name and I pound into her, emptying every last drop of cum inside her.

When she's stopped shaking, I lift my head and stare into her eyes. "Merry Christmas, baby."

"Merry Christmas," she breathes with a smile.

I roll onto my side, allowing Conor to slide in next to her so she's nestled between the two of us.

"I love you all so much," she mumbles sleepily as her eyes flutter closed.

"Shall we tell her what we want next Christmas?" Mikey asks with a chuckle.

"We'll tell her tomorrow," Shane says as he sits on the edge of the bed staring at her.

"I think we fucked her into a coma."

I have never seen my older brother so at peace in my whole life as he is when he's with her or our kids. But then she has the same effect on all of us. She is the light to our shade. The eye of our storm. Where we begin and end.

"God, she's fucking beautiful," Conor says with a soft sigh as he lays his head next to hers.

"She sure is," Mikey and I agree.

"Merry Christmas, boys," Shane says as he crawls into bed and lies next to me.

"Thank you for letting us bring her home," I whisper to him, remembering the day we found her hiding beneath a desk in a Russian gangster's mansion.

We were supposed to kill everyone in that house. But then we found her inside. It still makes me smile when I remember the way she fronted him. This pint-sized redhead in a hoody standing on her tiptoes to face off with my grumpy big brother.

"Thank you for making me, kid," he says with a wink.

THIRTEEN

Christmas Day

Today has been the most perfect day in the history of Christmases. Although they're a little young to fully understand, Ella and Finn loved tearing into their presents. And having their daddies and I playing with their new toys all morning made them squeal with laughter the entire time. We only had one tantrum from Ella when Conor stopped her from trying to climb the Christmas tree.

My husbands spoiled me with presents, even though I'd told them not to, making the cologne, socks and candy I got for them pale into insignificance.

I have a huge dopey grin on my face as I watch them now. Finn crawls to the sofa and reaches beneath it before putting something in his mouth.

My heart almost stops beating. "Oh, Jesus! Mikey!" I shout, pointing at our son. "He's chewing on the cock ring."

Mikey scoops Finn into his arms as he laughs loudly. "Aw he's enjoying it."

"Please take it off him," I say, wincing at our poor innocent child sucking on a sex toy.

"It's just a rubber ring. It doesn't become a cock ring until someone has actually worn it on their cock."

Conor walks up behind him and slaps Mikey lightly across the back of his head before taking Finn from his arms. "Stop saying 'cock' in front of my son," he says as he takes the offending item from Finn's grasp.

Our son's lower lip starts to tremble, but Conor swaps the ring for a rubber teething ring instead and Finn gnaws happily on it.

"It's Shane's fault for leaving his sex toys lying around the den," Mikey says, rubbing the back of his head.

"I will kick your ass Mikey," Shane says good naturedly as he walks up behind me and grabs a handful of my backside with his free hand while he holds Ella in his other arm. He bends his head low so he can whisper in my ear. "And I haven't forgotten about the spanking I owe you for that whole cock ring stunt, Mrs. Ryan."

A shiver of excitement skitters along my spine. "I said I was sorry," I whisper.

"Not good enough," he says with a wicked grin. "And I believe I get you all to myself next Thursday, right?"

My knees almost buckle as heat sears between my thighs. He's right. It's our date night next week. Just me and him.

"I'm gonna enjoy making you squirm so much, sweetheart," he growls before pressing a soft kiss on the nape of my neck and walking over to where Conor and Finn are sitting on the rug.

Mikey and Liam sit too. And then the six of them sit there, with smiles on their faces as my husbands talk and the babies play.

This is perfect.

Nothing could top this.

Nothing.

"Hey, Red, we were talking the other day about what we want for next Christmas," Mikey says and suddenly all eyes are on me. Even our children are looking at me.

"And what's that?" I ask, a hand on my hip as I wonder what devious scheme the four of them have concocted now.

They glance at each other, Mikey suddenly lost for words it seems.

"You tell her," Liam nudges Shane who rolls his eyes.

But then he looks at me and nods to Ella and Finn. "How about some more of these?"

ARE YOU READY FOR MORE?

There will be plenty more to come from Jessie and the Ryan brothers in 2023!

ALSO BY SADIE KINCAID

This is a novella connected to the New York Ruthless series, set after the end of Ryan Renewed. It is a dark Mafia, reverse harem romance which deals with adult themes including scenes of an explicit sexual nature.

If you haven't read the series yet, you can find them on Amazon and Kindle Unlimited

Ryan Rule

Ryan Redemption

Ryan Retribution

Ryan Reign

Ryan Renewed

New York Ruthless short stories can be found here

A Ryan Reckoning

A Ryan Rewind

A Ryan Halloween

Want to know more about The Ryan Brothers' buddies, Alejandro and Alana, and Jackson and Lucia? Find out all about them in Sadie's internationally bestselling LA Ruthless series. Available on Amazon and FREE in Kindle Unlimited.

Fierce King

Fierce Queen

Fierce Betrayal

Fierce Obsession

If you'd like to read about London's hottest couple. Gabriel and Samantha, then check out Sadie's London Ruthless series on Amazon. FREE in Kindle Unlimited.

Dark Angel

Fallen Angel

If you enjoy super spicy short stories, Sadie also writes the Bound series feat Mack and Jenna, Books 1, 2, 3 and 4 are available now.

Bound and Tamed

Bound and Shared

Bound and Dominated

Bound and Deceived

About the Author

Sadie Kincaid is a steamy romance author who loves to read and write about hot alpha males and strong, feisty females.

Sadie loves to connect with readers so why not get in touch via social media?

Join Sadie's reader group for the latest news, book recommendations and plenty of fun. Sadie's ladies and Sizzling Alphas

Sign up to Sadie's mailing list for exclusive news about future releases, giveaways and content here

Made in United States
Cleveland, OH
23 December 2024

12577040R00083